... *Arly Poole*

I spotted a hunk of mud at my feet, which I sure did want to pick up, to chuck at Roscoe Broda. Yet, I didn't. All I did was just stand there in the morning light and wish that I was anybody except who I'd got born to be. I just felt like a dumb and dirty boy, standing there, watching Addie Cooter cluck at her four mules, and see my daddy ride off to picking. He didn't wave to me, like usual. Mr. Broda followed the wagon on horseback and all I did was stand there, hurting inside for Papa.

I hated being Arly Poole.

Also by
ROBERT NEWTON PECK:

A Day No Pigs Would Die

ARLY

Robert Newton Peck

SCHOLASTIC INC.
New York Toronto London Auckland Sydney

No part of this publication may be reproduced in whole or in part, or stored in a retrieval system, or transmitted in any form or by any means, electronic, mechanical, photocopying, recording, or otherwise, without written permission of the publisher. For information regarding permission, write to Walker and Company, 720 Fifth Avenue, New York, NY 10019.

ISBN 0-590-43469-1

Copyright © 1989 by Robert Newton Peck. All rights reserved. Published by Scholastic Inc., 730 Broadway, New York, NY 10003, by arrangement with Walker and Company. POINT is a registered trademark of Scholastic Inc.

12 11 10 9 8 7 6 5 4 3 2 1   1 2 3 4 5 6/9

Printed in the U.S.A.   01

First Scholastic printing, November 1991

The author dedicates this book to another Florida author, a writer of excellent novels such as *Angel City* and *Forever Island*. His name is Patrick Smith. Hi Iris.

I also dedicate this book to a teacher who earned thirteen dollars a week in a one-room, dirt road school. Her clothes were as shabby as ours. Yet her torch guided us from the darkness, and our respect for her forever endures.

And to President Calvin Coolidge.

Robert Newton Peck

FLORIDA
1927

Property Pleasant Twp.
High School Media Center

FLORIDA
1977

Property Theatre Two
High School Media Center

CHAPTER 1

"Up," said Huff. "Move on up, Arly."

As I climbed a branch or two higher on the slanting oak limb, Huff Cooter followed. He was still on the downside of me.

"See anything?" he asked.

Squinting in the dark, I looked beyond the sprigs of swaying oak leaves toward the Lucky Leg. Some of the upstair rooms were black, but not all. One was lighted.

"Arly Poole," said Huff, "you gotta inch up a bit more, so's I can take a see for myself."

Earlier, it had been Huff Cooter's idea. Down on the ground it seemed to make more sense than away up here, where we were now. Huff's plan was to spy into the upper windows of the Lucky Leg Social Palace, and witness the dandies and the pretty ladies, all having at it. Seeing as it was Friday night, plenty ought to be in swing by this time. Some hot entertaining.

"Hey," I said, "I can see one of the gals. She's wearing a shiny green dress, with a slit up the side."

"What's she doing?" As he asked the question, Huff hustled up the oak limb almost to where I was hanging on real tight, so I wouldn't fall myself down and smack Florida.

A smile near about split my face before I gave Huff a tricky answer. "She's taking something off."

"*What?*" Huff hissed like a tomcat.

My grin near to hurt my face. "Oh, nothing you'd be itching to learn about."

"Come on, Arly. What's she taking off?"

"A gent's necktie."

Huff grunted a dirty word.

Long strands of gray moss was hanging down from the oak twigs, so we had to move our heads whenever the summer breeze made the moss sway. The rough oak bark was scratching my naked chest. Huff and I wore only trousers. Nothing else.

"Arly, what's the *guy* doing?"

"Well," I said, "right now he's smiling. But he looks more'n a bit nervous to be lonesome with her. He just walked over to see if their door was locked."

"Yeah," said Huff. "I bet so."

Here in Jailtown, the Lucky Leg was about the only public diversion. People say that the sporting carries on during the daytime too. The place was certain bubbling with fun right now. I could hear laughter and the clacking of pool balls. Several people talking all to once. And a man named Mr. Knuckle Knapp was playing a pink piano.

"What's she taking off now?" Huff wanted to know.

"An earring."

"Is that all?"

"Nope. She's also taking off her other one."

Huff crawled up to where I lay with my belly flat along the limb. He was trying to see over my rump and into the window.

"Which gal is it?" he asked.

"Flossie."

Huff moaned a low moan. "Boy, I gotta see her up close." He started to climb over me for a better view.

My hands tightened on the wood. "Careful, or you'll tumble the two of us, so's we'll fall and bust our necks."

"Yeah," he said, "it's Flossie all right. Ain't nobody in Jailtown with hair so sassy red."

As I looked, I noticed that Flossie's cheeks and lips were red too. Different shade. More like fire. Closing my eyes, I took a deep draw of air through my nose, hoping I'd smell a whiff of her perfume. No luck. All I got wind of was a sorry sniff of Huff Cooter. A picker smell. In Shack Row, where we lived, the Cooter family nested nearby to Papa and me. I'd smelt Cooters all of my life, almost twelve years, and them six Cooters had equal smelt us two Pooles.

"Look," said Huff, "she got one foot up on the edge of that fancy bed, and slipping off her garter. Yowie!"

"Hush," I warned him. "Else you'll invite Roscoe Broda's dogs to circle this tree, and bugle."

Huff punched my shoulder. "Don't you hush me none, Arly. I can lick you in a fistfight any time."

He was right. He could.

The bedroom window was less than a stone's throw away from us, so we could start to see plenty . . . until the light went out. Huff groaned. But somebody, and it was probable Flossie, struck a match. The candle flickered a breath or two and then pinpricked the gloom.

"Boy," whispered Huff, "I sure would like to be that lucky gentleman right now. Wouldn't you?"

"Sure would," I answered him, knowing certain well that neither Huff Cooter or Arly Poole were old enough to handle a high time with any of the pretty ladies at the Lucky Leg Social Palace. Both of us were only sneaking up on twelve.

Huff cussed again.

"I can't see much of Flossie. Can you?"

"Nope," Huff said.

"All we can make out is that there dandy with his necktie off. You reckon Miss Flossie is fixing to give her customer a great big kiss about sudden?"

"Arly, she's possible doing that and plenty else."

"What you suppose she's at?"

"Oh," said Huff, closing his eyes, "I got me a heavy hunch that Flossie's got her long red-painted fingernails running through his hair, like ten cooties."

Listening to Huff's colorful imagining, I leaned forward to push an inch or two closer to the open window. The katydids and crickets were whooping up so frequent that I couldn't hear a word of conversation. So I clung tight to that oak limb and pictured myself in the sweet arms of Miss Flossie. We didn't know whatever her family name was. Nobody at the Lucky Leg Social Palace announced more than a first name, except for Mr. Knuckle Knapp, and Miss Angel Free. The big blonde bosslady. She wasn't ever called just Angel. It was always Miss Angel.

Folks in Jailtown sometimes laughed, guessing that her name was the only *free* thing about Miss Angel. All else was for profit. Cash in advance.

"Huff, how much money do a man tote inside his pants pocket before he can as much as ring the Leg's front doorbell?"

Huff Cooter scratched himself. "Oh, I s'pose away up into the dollars. For sure, he'd best carry enough scratch to spread around, or Miss Angel will watch him git tossed into Okeechobee."

"Soon's we're twelve," I said, "you and me'll work as pickers and be earning men. I'll be fetching up melons and cukes right alongside of my daddy. On the labor docket that Mr. Roscoe Broda carries, it'll say Dan Poole, and then me, Arly Poole."

Huff spat. "Who wants to be a picker? We ain't hardly no better than colored folks. Far as I can figure, a picker ain't nothing but a white darky. Shack Row's all white people, like you Pooles and us Cooters. Yet nobody rise up nowhere, and no how. On account your daddy's like my mama. They'll both settle up the storekeeper every penny they sweat for."

Huff was right. Mrs. Stout'd claim it all. She'll squint down into that beat-up old ledger book and tell us we still owe. Shack rent eat up whatever it want. Nobody dare to say *liar* to anyone who worked for Captain Tant.

"Arly, can you spot any hot doings in some of the other windows?"

"No. All we can do is guess it."

Huff was silent for a spell. Then he spoke up. "Are you going to meet the boat when Sunday come?"

"Maybe. On account that the famous person is coming to town. Yet I certain don't know why anybody high and mighty would stop off here. I hope he throws a lot of pennies."

"Yeah," said Huff. "All to one fling."

Once a week, the Caloosahatchee Queen docked here in Jailtown, but not for long. The clean people only stood up, leaning on the railing, and pointed at us. I'd usual wave. Most always, some rich boatrider would fish a penny out of his pocket to toss into the lake. We kids'd dive to fetch it up. Some other kid always brung it up from the deep dock water. I'd not found it even a once time.

But I never quit trying.

CHAPTER 2

The scream woke me up.

Opening my eyes, I rubbed my face with both hands and stared up at the roof of our shack. It was easy to tell by the roof holes that night was near over. A peacock screeched again, making me wonder how so pretty a bird could cry out such a smart awful noise.

"Papa," I said, "it's time to shake out."

A few steps away, on the other mattress tick, my daddy was still asleep, breathing heavy like always.

His sleeping sounded stiffer than a sore back.

Rolling off my tick, I heard the straw inside it whisper, as if to warn me that it'd soon make another Florida morning and the picker wagon would be here to lug folks to the field. And if Papa missed the wagon, he'd have to run or get fined by the field boss, Mr. Roscoe Broda.

"Papa," I said, shaking the bony shoulder that was under his work shirt, "it's soon morning."

He sat up. "Dang," I heard him mumble, "it's like I just went down, Arly boy."

"The wagon'll be coming. You wash up while I fix your eats." The dirt of the floor was cool under my bare feet as I poked up the cook stove to a boil. Dan Poole liked hot tea at sunup because it loosened his joints. To be a picker and do stoop work, a man had to make his back bend easy. Papa weren't very big in any direction, up or out.

As it was turning light outside, I hoped he'd hustle himself some, so's he wouldn't be last in line to load onto the picker wagon. Papa pulled off his shirt to wash at the bucket, and his white chest loomed out like a skinny lantern. His arms and face were red and he looked the way most pickers looked, like he'd lost every fight in his life. And that he had never knowed shade.

Outside, the peacocks nagged at each other under the custard apple trees. I was praying that my daddy wouldn't nag me about where Huff and I'd gone last night. And final fell out a tree.

"Hear that?" I said. "Them peacocks realize the mules coming with the wagon. So you best hurry, hear?"

Papa mussed up my hair. "Yup, I hear it, Arly. Don't guess I'd make rising if'n we didn't have them peacocks around." He pulled his shirt over his thin hair.

"They sure sound ugly, don't they? Even uglier than old Captain Tant hisself."

Resting a hand over my mouth, Papa said, "No, boy, you don't sass thataway on the Captain. He's hard. But he ain't near ornery as Roscoe Broda, folks say, so you better don't badlip him none. A mean mouth spoons in trouble, Arly. Faith me on it."

He drank his tea and bit into a flour biscuit faster than a hungry gator. I was glad to see him eat two biscuits instead of his usual single. While he ate, I stuffed a cooked potato and our last strip of dried hog meat into his noon bag, and then knotted the neck so's his food wouldn't foul gritty with field dust.

"Be sure to rest your bag in the shade," I told him, "so's it'll keep proper and won't spoil out."

A mule snorted. Papa jumped, a late look on his face. He didn't cotton to be last in Mr. Roscoe Broda's line.

"We best hurry, Papa. Real sudden."

"Yeah, we do."

After I near to pushed him out of our door, together we run up the dusty ground, along the line of shacks. Everbody run, afeared to be late. All I could think of was that I didn't want Dan Poole to be the last man to crawl over the tailgate. Papa couldn't run too fast, so I about dragged him with both my hands hauling to his one. I wanted to work in his place; but rules was rules, about the count of pickers that got took. They didn't usual use nobody eleven.

A mule let out a long series of hee-haws, a sound that worked back and forth, cutting through the gray of morning like a bucksaw. Up ahead, I saw Addie Cooter, the big woman who drive the picker wagon, holding the ribbons to the four mules.

I liked Huff's mama. Papa did too, because she'd bring drinking water to the vegetable fields, ever workday. She had a big body that near filled the wagon bench and her face usual scratched a big smile to go with it. She was our nearby neighbor in Shack Row. Addie Cooter had five kids. And claimed she'd popped four before she'd knowed what caused it.

When I waved to Mrs. Cooter she waved back, motioning with a frown and a toss of her head that I'd best get Papa loaded on quick.

"Hurry up, Papa."

His lungs were heaving in air, but those bandy old legs kept a trot to his feet. I could see we'd make the tailgate and he'd not be the last one to skin aboard. Papa let loose of my hand and run for it. Roscoe Broda stood at the tailgate of the picker wagon, holding his roster board under one of his bully arms. Roscoe wasn't fat. He was just built solid as a plow ox. When he eyed Papa, he spat into the dust of the wagon ruts.

"Arly Poole," said Addie, from up on her wagon seat, "you best look yourself tidy come tomorrow." She said it righteous bold, as if she didn't care a sniff if Mr. Broda heard her say it.

"Yes'm, Mrs. Cooter."

I was thankful to see that Papa wasn't going to load on last, because old Dinker Witt was a good twenty steps back of Papa, limping along on his twisted knee. Mr. Witt put an eye to Roscoe Broda's big boot, like he knew he'd load on last and take whatever meanness come due.

But then I saw Papa drop his noon bag.

He run a couple-three steps beyond it, looking at Roscoe as if he couldn't decide whether to go back and fetch it or miss eating until sundown. Quicker than a spooked rabbit, I made a dive into the dust for the sack and got to it just as Papa did, making him fumble it again. Our four hands seemed to tie into a knot.

"Hurry," I said.

Ahead of us, Dinker Witt threw his lame old body up and over the tailgate and into Addie's wagon bin, joining the twenty others already aboard. This meant that Papa would be last and he'd have to work at half pay.

Roscoe Broda put a mark on his roster sheet and said, "Dan Poole," in a voice deeper than dirt. "Half wages for Saturday."

Papa tried to hasten over the tailgate, but he couldn't move fast enough. Roscoe whipped a kick into my daddy's backside, making Papa sprawl into the floor of the wagon bin. A few of the pickers reached out hands to help him up and made a place for him on the long bench boards.

I knew it was the rule.

The kick was sorry enough, but the half wages for a whole day's work would hurt us Pooles a lot meaner when we had to trade at Mrs. Stout's store in Jailtown. Captain Tant own the store. Just like he most own everthing on earth, even the peacocks that he'd brought here. And people usual said he charge the tourist folks ten cents a bag to feed 'em. I'd once saw a city lady fish out a dime so her kid could feed the peacocks. Like ten cents was nothing.

Dan Poole would have to sweat bent over in the cucumbers all day for not much more than ten cents, at half wages.

I spotted a hunk of mud at my feet, which I sure did want to pick up, to chuck at Roscoe Broda. Yet I didn't. All I did was just stand there in the morning light and wish that I was anybody except who I'd got born to be. I just felt like a dumb and dirty boy, standing there, watching Addie Cooter cluck at her four mules, and see my daddy ride off to picking. He didn't wave to me, like usual. Mr. Broda followed the wagon on horseback and all I did was stand there, hurting inside for Papa.

I hated being Arly Poole.

CHAPTER 3

Huff showed up.

We stood behind the row of gray shacks tossing bits of bark and loose rock into Lake Okeechobee, listening to the *plunk* sound.

"We was lucky last night," he said.

"How so?"

"First off, because we didn't hurt ourselfs when we tumble off the tree. Second, we didn't let Roscoe's men see us, or hear us neither. If so, we'd got whupped for sure."

"But we didn't see much of Flossie and the necktie sport she was socializing."

Huff agreed. "No, I don't guess we did."

"Hey, do you want to walk over to the cane crusher, and see if maybe they're shorthanded at the sugar mill?"

"Won't do no good," Huff answered, throwing a pebble to the quiet morning lake water. "Until you're twelve, nobody'll take you on. Captain's orders. And it's Captain Tant or Roscoe Broda that'll decide when you're twelve. If'n we're thick enough, we'll sudden be on the labor docket. No questions asked about birthdays."

As I sat in the dust, my back against the trunk of a custard apple tree, I looked up at my friend. "My daddy say that when Sunday come, that's tomorrow, things'll bound to change."

Huff shook his head.

"No famous outsider is gonna do squat. Captain owns Jailtown. Nobody else." Huff sighed. "I seen the old Captain one time. He got white hair. Walks with a cane, he do. A mite bended over. But he wearing a white suit of clothes. Clean as a cloud. And sporting white shoes."

"Did ya run?"

"Yeah," said Huff, "but not until Captain look right at me with those burny eyes of his. Fever eyes, my mama calls 'em. It was sort of like meeting up with God."

I laughed. "God don't pay visits to Jailtown. But come tomorrow, a famous person is due on the Queen."

"Arly, I believe it when I see it happen. Folks aplenty git off the Caloosahatchee Queen at the town dock. But they seem always to git back up that gangplank and leave with the boat whistle."

Leaving where we live, Shack Row, the pair of us head toward Jailtown with the hopes of maybe earning a dime, or even a nickel. We took the shortcut, the one only us picker kids use, because so much of the path was through muddy water. Shoe people didn't use it.

Of all the sights to see in Jailtown, perhaps the only, the one that captured a stranger's eye, would be the big lady's leg atop the Lucky Leg Social Palace. It stood up taller than a shack. Twice as tall, and painted a blushy pink color of female flesh. Covering most of it was a see-through black lace stocking, wove out of real rope, like a catfish net. The rope was coal black. Yet the wide garter that held it up was redder than raw.

As we walked close to the front door, I spotted Miss Angel Free and her silvery-gold hair, dressed in orange satin. Yawning, she was saying a goodnight to a pair of customers, using a sugary voice.

"Come again, gentlemen," she said. "At my place, we're sort of akin to an Irish tenor's mouth." She giggled. "We never close."

Miss Angel Free continued to smile until the two dredgers tipped their hats to her, turned their backs, and final went stumbling along the red dust of Jailtown's main street. Her smile quickly faded and she spat over the porch rail.

Seeing the two of us kids, Huff and me, her face twisted into a hurried frown.

"Beat it," she told us. "If'n I catch either one of you young tomcats within a sniff of this establishment, I'll ask Mr. Broda to sic his redtick hounds after you, and chase you into swamp."

As she cussed at us, waving her arm to spook us away, I could hear the many bracelets rattling on her arm. It was said that Miss Angel own over a hundred bracelets, and each one a gift from an admiring man. They was, I was thinking, a lot to admire with Miss Angle Free. She was about twice the size of Flossie.

Huff and I trotted away.

When we stopped, Huff said, "Miss Angel don't own the Leg."

"She don't?"

"Naw. Captain own it. Old Captain Tant own everthing, near about." He pointed across the dirt street at Mrs. Stout's trading store, a place where Papa would have to report to, ever Saturday at sundown, to collect his wages. "Captain own the store too."

There was usual no wages to collect. Somehow us Pooles fell into owing, so the debt and our shack rent ate up what little Dan Poole had sweat to earn for six days. You couldn't leave Jailtown in debt. It was one of Captain's rules. Once in a spell, a man would try to run off. But there wasn't no safety to reach. Lake on one side. A swamp on two. The swamp held some gators longer than a wagon. The alligators, jaws and all, would treat you kinder than Broda's dogs.

One night, some years ago, Papa had got hisself more'n a mite shiny on moon, and had whispered secrets he knew to me. About how, a long time ago, Miss Angel had been a kiss or two closer than cozy to Captain Tant. My daddy warned me that I wasn't ever to repeat it.

I didn't. Not even to Huff Cooter.

"Gee," said Huff, "I sort of hoped we could say a howdy to Flossie." Looking back over his shoulder at the Lucky Leg, he added, "But I don't guess Miss Angel would allow her to talk to picker kids. Not if she's watching."

Flossie was one of the few ladies we knew by name. But that was all.

Ruby and Amber were two others, but Flossie was our favorite lady to say hello to. Then we'd run into the swamp and giggle. Only one time did the pair of us ever work up the gumption for chatter. That was the day Flossie had just arrived in Jailtown and was crying, on account she was homesick. It'd be the only time in her entire life that she'd strayed off from home. She talked to us about her little sister and her dog. Then told us how old she was.

Flossie was thirteen.

It wasn't Flossie I was sweet on. Instead, I had feelings for Huff's older sister, Essie May. In all, there was five Cooter children. But really only four. Anybody man or boy, who looked at Essie May Cooter knowed right away sudden that she wasn't no child. At thirteen, Essie was a small woman.

Huff and I moved through town. We had secret routes, in shadows, along board fences and through alleys, that kept us hid from view. We avoided people who wore shoes on their feet. Shoe people were rich folks, my daddy warned me. Men in shoes could hire you, fire you, tell you where to go, how to live, what to breathe and eat and think. So I never looked at a stranger's face first. It was always his feet. If a man wore shoes, or big boots, I didn't dare look up at his face. Because I was too afraid. I looked down.

Huff found a pack of CAMEL cigarettes. They'd gotten wet, turned brown, and their owner had throwed them away. As Huff usual carried matches, we hid underneath an empty house and puffed ourselfs silly.

Butting out his smoke, Huff swore. "Dang it," he told me. "I just figured out that old Captain Tant even own that pretty little Flossie gal. He own her outright. Miss Angel Free bosses her at the Lucky Leg, but it be Captain who own her, mind and soul."

His face seemed to be so sad as he was sharing his thoughts. It was as though his own secret candle had sudden blowed out.

"Captain Tant own the jail," said Huff. "And he own the judge, Jailor Jim Tinner. Own it all. Name me one thing around here that old Captain don't hold a claim on. Name me one free thing, Arly."

"Huff," I said, "the Captain don't own *me*."

CHAPTER 4

"You hungry, Arly?"

My stomach jumped to Huff's question, so I told him I was. "Sort of. Got anything in your pockets?"

"Nope." Huff grinned. "Fact is, these here pants don't *got* no pockets. Let's push over to the dock and see if'n we can scare up some catfish."

We started on our way, rounded a corner, and saw the lake. Out across Okeechobee seemed like the end of the world, and where the distant waterline met the sky it looked like one got seamed to the other.

"Catfishing sure is a business around here," said Huff. "You wonder who eats it all."

My belly was so empty I near told Huff that I could eat a catfish raw. Catfish in Okeechobee be good-size, fatter than prosperous, and some of the whoppers balance near as much as a dog on the weighing scales.

Fishcamps was ample plenty, so folks told it, all along the lake banks, as well as up into the dead rivers. People called 'em dead because they didn't seem to go nowheres. Folks at the fishcamps be city men mostly, trying to booze it up, play poker, and maybe hook a keeper. Some of the city gents fetched along costly gear, poles and reels that was worth as dear as way up into dollars. Huff and I used beanpoles, or a stalk of cane would do; and for a float bobber, the corky woodpulp of a custard apple served out really fine. At least the catfish never seem to fuss over it.

"Ain't no better meal than a slice of Okeechobee catfish," Huff said. "So, seeing I don't guess we got us hooks or heave lines, let's go find Brother."

"Suits me."

We found him. He was setting his dock, mending a seine. It had sinkers along one edge and floats lining the other. The net was in his lap and over his beefy legs. Even seated, Brother Smith was taller than I was standing. He was a giant, the only colored man that got treated decent. Even the white folks spoke to him . . . all except Captain. Brother Smith's hair be as gray as his shirt and pants. He never wore no shoes.

"Well," he said in his soft voice, looking at me and Huff. "Hither ye be."

Brother Smith talked like a Bible, people enjoyed saying. Folks said he was neighbor close to God and would still be so even if he hadn't been a fisherman. Jailtown didn't have a church or a preacher, but Brother Smith come righteous close to serving the settlement on both counts. He was, I reckoned, near to big as a church and about as holy as any man, dead or alive, or any lady. Holier, I figured, than a few of the ladies with the red lips who worked for Miss Angel Free back in the Lucky Leg Social Palace.

"Bless you, brothers," said Brother. He called all men *brother*, which is how he earn his nickname.

"And bless you too, Brother Smith," said Huff. He really meant it, I knew. Whenever I was with Brother, I just felt cleaner and stronger than usual. Most folks did. When someone die in Jailtown, white pickers as well as black sent for Brother Smith, so he'd utter sweet words over the grave in the muck soil. I'd never honest seed a church, or been inside one, but the sound of holy music couldn't ring out any more saintly than the deep voice of Brother Smith's.

I'd heared that, years and years back, Captain Tant's daughter had fell herself out a boat and into Okeechobee, and it be Brother Smith who'd dived in and pulled her to shore. That was how come Brother didn't have to live in Darky Town no more, but had a place to his own. Even so, Brother Smith wanted a church built, but Captain Tant be dead set against it. He didn't allow no churches at all. But over in Darky Town, the colored people sang hymns after the sun rested down.

Pulling his dwindle stick from a knot in his seine, Brother Smith pointed it at Jailtown's biggest boat dock. "Tomorrow," he said, "the big boat be here."

"Is it true that you're a prophet?" Huff Cooter asked Brother.

The big man filled his lungs, looked at the brace of us, and let out a long sigh like he was thinking on it. "No, I a fisher, like Simon. I be no prophet. Yet I know a famous person come, as sure as John Baptist knowed about Jesus."

"Captain'll be mad," said Huff.

"Maybe so," Brother Smith said, "but ol' Captain ain't young no more." As he talked, Brother pointed a finger in a gentle way. "Captain's getting long of tooth."

"What's that mean?"

Brother smiled. "Olden. Like me."

"Say, what kind of a knot is that you're twisting into your net?" Huff asked.

"This?" Brother Smith tapped the twine with his

dwindle. "It ain't got a name, like Huff and Arly do. So I calls it a hemplock."

"Did you create it, Brother?"

His big black face lit up brighter than a Coleman lantern. "No," he said, poking the dwindle in my ribs, gentle easy. "I just invent it. Because only Almighty God create."

I saw Brother rest a large paw on Huff's shoulder and then his other on mine. "Out yonder," he said, turning us around to look at the water, "out in Okeechobee, I hook me a catfishy. But I couldn't never create one. Hadn't I seen one, I never could've thunk up a creation. Young brothers, an ol' catfish favors you an' me. A fish and boy be only two of God's ideas."

As I listened to Brother Smith's deep voice almost whispering between my ear and Huff's, I kept on squinting into the sun and the silver it dropped out on Okeechobee. Big as the sea it was, folks said, and in a storm, everyone in Jailtown agree, only a fool would dare to cross. And he'd possible never come back. Because he'd make food for catfish, gars, and gators.

"Brother, how did the lake git here?" I asked our big friend.

"Come," he answered, "and maybe I can show you young brothers how it begin."

The three of us walked along the short dock, Brother Smith in the middle, dragging the big seine net over one beefy shoulder, which he then hanged up on pegs that he'd pound into the gray boards of his boat house. At our feet, the shore was sandy in one spot, so Brother bended to it. We hunker down to look.

"Long ago," said Brother, his fingers smoothing the sand, "the land be flat as firmament. But then God dip the tip of one finger into the Florida dirt, like so, to dent a great hole and that be Okeechobee."

I couldn't breathe. "Praise be," I final said, staring at the lake. "The tip of God's finger do all *that?*"

It weren't easy to measure just how big the Almighty really was. A whole lot bigger than Brother Smith. Too big for my mind to fetch in.

"Brother," I asked him, "how big's the world? I actual want to know."

He shaked his gray head. "Me, I don't know at all." His hand reached upward into the sunlight like he could touch beyond it. Then he walked away from the lake shore, as we followed, to where we could rest in the shade of a small stand of scrub pine. I watched his fingers pry off a bark slab and then point to the lighter scar of underbark that now showed on the trunk.

"Children always want knowing how big our world be," he told us. "But under each chip of bark live a tiny town, all style of life in yonder, too small to see. Or hear. I guess it be there all right. A tiny town of life."

"You mean like Jailtown?"

Brother nodded. "Almost exact. So I say to you, young brothers, not to ask only how big our world be. Ask how small it go."

Wrinkling his nose, Huff Cooter leaned in close by the bark scar on the trunk of the pine and squinted. "I can't see no little town."

Brother Smith whispered to him. "And nobody in that little town see you. Or care how growed you is. In there, they got their own business, and catfish to cook up for supper."

"God made that little town too?"

The big face grinned. "Easy," said Brother. "As easy as the Lord poked a fingertip hole for Okeechobee."

"I don't believe it," Huff snorted. "God really built a tiny little town inside here?" His finger tapped the trunk. "A entire little town?"

Brother nodded. "As if He had nothin' else to do."

CHAPTER 5

"**W**hoa still," Papa ordered me.

Once again, like he'd just do over and over, he dip our hairbrush in the water bucket and attack my thicket of hair. His tongue peek out from one corner of his mouth.

"I ought to barber it," Papa said to my hair, "on account it's overgrowed."

"We don't have time. The boat's due."

He nodded. As he brushed me, I looked at his hair, thin and gray, with an ample of white in it. But he'd comb it down and part it proper, a doing that I hadn't seen my daddy bother at for years.

"There," he said, straightening his back. "Now put on your hat and we'll head along."

"How do I look?"

"Passable."

I smiled at him. "Good as Sunday?"

"Right," he said, tossing the brush into the corner of the shack next to his bed tick. "I want you lookin' your best today, Arly."

As we walked along Shack Row, pointed toward the Jailtown dock, I liked wearing my hat. It was white, with a dark blue ribbon around it for a band. Usual I wore it only on the Four of July. But today be special. As we walked, I know my hat was getting a bit too small for my head. It fitted rightly snug. Yet I felt proud to wear it, because Papa had bought it for me. My hat had cost fifteen cents.

"Morning to ya, Daniel." The voice that had called out Papa's name had chirp out from the smiling face of our neighbor, Addie Cooter. All six Cooters were headed for town. Essie May too. I tried not to stare at Essie May Cooter. Yet I usual did, even if she be a year or more older than I was.

"The same to ya, Mrs. Cooter," Papa said back with a wave.

She shook a warning finger. "How many times I gotta warn ya, Dan Poole, to call me Addie? I can't abide a handsome man like you to address me as Mrs. Cooter."

I winked at Huff and he winked back, as all eight of us joined the parade of people in Jailtown. It was Sunday and some local folks sure did honor it. Dressed up brighter than Christmas, and that included the ladies who usual abided inside the Lucky Leg Social Palace.

The Lucky Leg ladies wore red aplenty on their lips, like they slapped it on with a trowel. I notice Huff Cooter grin as he looked at Miss Angel in her bright green satin dress, trimmed with white lace. Even her fan was green, to match. She sure was a stepper.

We all headed for the boat dock, the very biggest one in town, to greet the Sunday boat that usual come across Okeechobee from Belle Glade. Folks said the steamer sometimes stopped at Pahokee and that it would today, to pick up our famous lady so's she could cross the lake to Jailtown.

"I wonder," I told Huff, "if Captain Tant will

show today. Or will he just stay in his big gingerbread house and not care."

His mother answered my wondering. "Captain won't come." Her voice lowered. "Mr. Tant don't want this stranger here. Neither do Broda. But I do know who put up some money for the boat ticket."

Papa raised an eyebrow. "Who?"

Mrs. Cooter moved her big body a step closer to where Papa stood, as we'd found a strip of shade next to a cane warehouse wall. "I heard tell it was Miss Liddy."

Nobody in Jailtown mention Miss Liddy Tant a whole lot. She was Captain's daughter. Folks said she was to get wed one time, years and years ago, to one of the plume hunters who'd come to Okeechobee to gun down egrets. But no wedding ever took place, because Captain Tant got Miss Liddy's boyfriend spook off, or killed. Anyhow, he got took out in a fish boat and never brought back.

"You know," I heard Addie Cooter whisper to my daddy's ear, "they say that them two, Captain and Miss Liddy, live in their big ol' house and don't never speak a word to one another."

"Is that true?" Papa asked.

"Gospel. That poorly woman ain't been seen out of doors in a whole sack of seasons. Some say not since the tragedy. And you want to know who told me?"

My father nodded.

"Roscoe. Between you and me, Dan Poole, I always had me a hunch that Roscoe Broda would up and wed Miss Liddy Tant and has felt thataway since before Noah's flood. He never married, ya know. Still lone. I figure Roscoe's forty and Miss Liddy's ten year older. But he'd wed her tomorrow if the chance come ripe."

Papa grunted. "Love's a circus."

I saw Addie Cooter poke Papa with her hand.

"Love," she said, "ain't got nothin' to do with Roscoe's courting Miss Liddy. It's the land he's after. And I figure both Captain and his daughter can see right through Roscoe Broda, and I'm dang glad they do."

"Hey, there's the judge," Huff said.

Sure enough, there he was, in his Sunday black suit, mopping his round face with a square hanky. Jailor Jim Tinner wasn't what the folks in town called him out loud. To his face, they usual called him Judge Tinner, or just Judge. He was the official law in Jailtown. Judge Tinner also got put in charge, by Captain, of running our jail. And whenever there was enough prisoners to form up a road gang, Judge took to be boss of the chainers. Some said he was a lawyer.

Addie Cooter curled her lip.

"Well," she said in a low voice to Papa, "there's our law. Roscoe told me a sorry tale. He says that it's mostly moonshiners that rot in the jailhouse, on account of Judge not wanting them to cut in on the whiskey he run hisself."

A small black dot appear away out on the straight line of one blue meeting another, in the middle of Lake Okeechobee. People straighted arms and point fingers. Kids got lifted up on shoulders.

I heared a steamer whistle.

CHAPTER 6

"**I** gotta get off my feet," Addie said.

Looking down, I saw Mrs. Cooter's old scuffy shoes, hot as it was. It be a caution shame, I was thinking, if she'd saved up and bought 'em too small at Mrs. Stout's.

Lots of folks, I had sort of figure out, tried wearing shoes, or boots. Papa had shoes on. His work boots. They didn't shine up too prosperous, even though he'd earlier yank a rag to 'em, before we'd left our shack. All five of the Cooter kids was barefoot, like me. I'd guess that about half the town people was shod that Sunday, and most be the grown folks.

Out on Okeechobee, the steamer boat seem to be taking her own time, as if she weren't too itching to visit Jailtown. However, lots of people had gather to greet the boat and take a fresh look-see at the famous visitor.

Huff Cooter sighed. "Sure wish that ol' boat would whip herself along."

"Yeah," I told him. "Me too."

It was right then I heared people start to mumble. Heads turning around, away from the lake, and eyes all look in one direction. That was when I saw a very thin lady, dressed in white lace. Her face was paler than yesterday's death, more gray than pink, and her hands weren't much more meaty than twigs. Over her head was a parasol which served to keep her shaded more than the rest of us. The lady stood quietly on the dock.

She look different.

Most of the people in Jailtown looked the same. We were pickers, catfishers, gator and plume hunters, fur skinners, cane mill workers, some growers who own citrus, black people and white, dredgers along with their wives and children, along with a few Seminoles who kept to themselves.

"Who's that?" a woman ask.

Her husband whisper his answer. "Holy Moses," he told her, "that's Miss Liddy Tant."

"Ain't possible," someone else said. "Captain's against us." And then another voice mention something called the Rural Education Act.

A few people spoke to Miss Liddy Tant, bowing as they done so. She mere nod in return. But then she did bother to speak to one person, the somebody who'd long ago saved her life.

"Good morning, Brother Smith."

He quick took off his hat and smiled. "Good morning to you, Missy Tant."

She stood her ground, pale and proud, and waited as the Caloosahatchee Queen blowed her whistle again, three times, and creep close enough to the dock for me to see the faces of the city people who lean on her rail. They waved to us and we all waved back. Nobody throwed pennies.

"Papa," I asked, "are them fancy people coming just to see Jailtown? Or to see the Leg?"

He shook his head. "I don't guess so. They say the Caloosahatchee Queen be a day boat, and the people on board is sightseers. She stops here to take on wood fuel, then goes to Moore Haven and back to Belle Glade where she moors up. A few'll go see the Lucky Leg."

Two black men dressed up as sailors pushed a gangplank to our dock. Miss Liddy walked forward, and as she went to meet the steamer, people made a path for her, backing off. She looked leaner than a dryspell pea pod.

"God bless ya, Miss Liddy," Addie Cooter said, and Miss Liddy flashed her a faint smile.

Plenty of people got off the boat.

Which one, I wondered, was the famous person? I certain couldn't tell. City people all look the same to me. They looked *new*, not like they was used stuff to buy in Mrs. Stout's store. Compared to the city sight-seers, Papa just plain looked wore out. People in Jail-town seem to be old, tired, and dirty, in spite of washing up for Sunday.

The last person to walk down the gangplank off the Caloosahatchee Queen was a very small woman.

She wasn't old, but she sure didn't look fresh-painted like the girls from the Lucky Leg, the ones who would sometimes wave to Huff or to me, and blow us kisses. The little lady carried a flowered carpetbag by its handle, but the flowers on the cloth seem to fade out most of their color.

"Papa," I asked, "could *she* be our famous visitor?"

He nodded. "I think you're right, Arly."

Only one person went to greet her, and that was Miss Liddy Tant. The rest of us just sort of moved out from the shade, to get up real close, and see it for ourselfs. Papa and I ducked between people to hear it all, right up front. Miss Liddy Tant talk up first.

"Miss Binnie Hoe?"

The new lady smiled. "Yes, I am."

"I am Liddy Tant. Welcome to Jailtown."

The two ladies shook hands, and I hear the famous lady say, "I'm here because of you, Miss Tant, and because of President Coolidge."

Miss Tant nod to a man in the crowd who rush up to carry Miss Hoe's belongings. Everything was real calm and quiet. I saw Miss Hoe look us all over, yet she didn't snicker, the way the city tourists did. Another man come over to hand Miss Hoe a tumbler of what looked like a lemon drink. Thanking him, she took a sip, and I saw her face tighten. As she swallow with a bit of effort, a gang of men busted out laughing. And I sudden knowed why.

So did Papa.

"They spiked it," he said. "Put a stick of moon in it, as a joke." His voice had a sorry to it, like what they done to her weren't funny.

I figured Miss Hoe would spit out the whiskey, but she didn't. In fact, she took another modest pull from the glass, which near to shock the pants off me, as well as the dredger men.

"Thank you, sir," Miss Hoe said to the rowdy bunch of dredgers to which the giver of the drink had returned. "If I am to flourish here in Jailtown, I'm sure that I shall need more than one swallow of such . . . spirited fortification." Her voice sounded strong, like it come right up her spine and out her mouth.

I saw the one dredger's face redden. But then he grin, and with a wide sweep of his beefy arm, he gave Miss Hoe a right courtly bow. Some of the dredgers even clapped.

"Tomorrow," said Miss Hoe, "at eight o'clock, I shall begin my day as Jailtown's first schoolteacher."

I looked at Papa. "She's a . . . *schoolteacher*? But you said we'd have a famous somebody. All we get is some old lady schoolteacher. Jailtown don't have no school."

Papa nodded. "I know, Arly. But maybe, now that she's here, we'll have one."

Miss Hoe was looking around at all of us. "All right," she said, "who will volunteer to be my first pupil? I will teach people of all ages."

No person moved. It was like we was froze up, or half dead. I didn't even breathe. No one dare to budge a step forward and sign up for school, and I sure didn't want to be first. Never, my daddy had warn me, ever be first or last in line for anything. That was when I saw Miss Liddy nod to Brother Smith, like she knowed folks would follow his lead. Brother then edge his way through the crowd until he stop face to face with Miss Hoe. Holding his hat, his big voice spoke out gentle and low.

"They call me Brother Smith," he said, bowing.

The famous lady stared up at him, as if almost suspecting that he'd pick her up to slip into his shirt pocket.

"Please to meet you, Mr. Smith," said the little woman. "My name is Binnie Hoe. And so you would like to attend school."

Brother nodded. "Yes'm. Before I die, Missy Hoe, I aim to read Bible, clear through. Can you please learn a old fisher like me to read?"

"Yes," she said, "I really can."

There was a mumble in the crowd of white folks, like they sure didn't cotton to have a colored man like Brother Smith talking up first to a white lady. Even if he be somebody sort of holy special in Jailtown. Papa nudged me a step closer to where Miss Binnie Hoe was standing. She weren't no taller than me. Next to Brother Smith, Miss Hoe looked no bigger than a chigger bug. Then, from behind my back, Papa pushed me.

"Take off your hat, Arly."

CHAPTER 7

Sunday night turned out a whooper.

Most of the doings got perform by Papa and Mrs. Addie Cooter, on account they both seem to fall into a celebration mood. Addie roast a gator tail and some catfish over a outdoor fire while Papa boil some collards. He sang as he cooked.

"How come you're so joyful?" I asked him.

"On account," Papa took a breath, "that our famous lady actual did come to Jailtown. She really git here. A genuine schoolteacher."

"Amen," said Addie.

Mrs. Cooter had squirrel away a jug of tart apple wine which got shared to many a mouth. I sneak a sip. To me it tasted right sour, sort of like trying to drink a hot fork. Dinker Witt and his wife come to join us, but neither of them cared to nip at Addie's jug, because both Mr. and Mrs. Witt claim they once be church people who didn't cotton to spirits.

Mrs. Yurman had a pan of leftover pickle juice and that got poured over the collard greens. We had salt too, enough to sprinkle everybody's turnips. It sure turned out to be a fancy feeding. Best of all, I got to sit beside Essie May Cooter.

Papa raked his mouth with a shirt sleeve. "Arly boy, that's cooking fit for a Sunday."

"Sure was," I told him.

"We ain't had us a jubilee here in Shack Row for a bunch of season," Papa told me. "No sir. But today, on this here Sunday evening, we got ourselfs more'n hope to be grateful about."

I swallowed fish. "You mean that teacher lady?"

Papa nodded. "Sure certain do." As he come closer to where I sat, next to Essie, I could smell the apple wine on his breath. "Remember how I had to shove you forward?"

I recall it real clear. It happen right after Brother done it. Using both hands, Papa had near pushed me hard enough to beach a boat, right toward the Miss Hoe lady, close enough to smell how clean she be. Not like Mrs. Cooter or Mrs. Witt. Looking at her made my hands sweat a mite. Besides, I sure didn't cotton to the idea of school.

Glancing over at Addie Cooter made me recollect how she usual smelled of mules. But that weren't too bad, on account that a mule smell better than a field picker.

Jumping up into the air, Papa landed and then kick the dust. "Hot dang!" he hooted. "Arly boy is gonna git schooling. The lady said he could report tomorrow morn." He spun around in a happy circle. "Golly, I could spit and hit the moon."

As he danced a clog in the dusty road which ran between the two rows of shacks, the people were laughing, like they was fixing to enjoy his fun. When he final quit his jigging, Dan Poole was short of breath, yet it didn't sober his grin. Nary a mite.

Papa raise both hands to the sky. "Hey, we oughta spirit ourselfs on some music. Dinker," he said to Mr

Witt, "how about fetching that old busted-up fiddle of yourn, and scratch us all a tune?"

Mr. Witt limp off to his shack and then return with a fiddle under his arm.

"I don't guess I've ever want to dance myself dizzy more'n I do right to moment," Papa said.

While old Dinker Witt was tuning his strings with a thumb, and twisting his stick tighter, Papa prance over to Addie Cooter, a woman who be ample large enough to make two of him. Maybe even three. He bent a bow to her, real gracious, and begged her for a dance.

"Mercy," Addie told him, "I ain't been asked to dance for half of my lifetime, Dan Poole. Ya don't got no notion what you're possible in for."

"No matter," Papa told her. "On account you can probable dance lots fancier than I can breathe."

Everyone laughed.

Mr. Witt struck up *Turkey in the Straw*, which start Papa and Mrs. Cooter to dancing. It was surprising that Addie Cooter could fling herself around so light. Maybe it was because she'd earlier took off her shoes and was barefoot.

"I'd like to dance too," Essie May said, looking straight at me as she spoke. "Arly, let's do."

"Well," I told her, "I don't guess I'm too fancy at it."

"I'll learn ya."

Standing before me was Essie May Cooter. A bit taller than I be, and rounder, but still slender. Graceful as a willow in wind. Long hair, bright eyes, wearing nothing but a little white dress, with a ruffle or two, looking sweeter than a sugar biscuit. Gently she took my hand. As she done it, I promised to remember this for the rest of my life.

thing I knowed, Essie May Cooter and I was

prancing around like we really understood what we was doing. And I didn't give a hoot if Essie was a mite taller than me. Essie was laughing and I was too. Sure was fun. Huff Cooter was clicking a pair of spoons, like bones, keeping time to Mr. Witt's fiddle playing.

Papa quit for breath. When the music stopped too, I heared him tell Mrs. Cooter, "I don't recall ever feeling so doggone happy. Except when Arly got born."

I knowed Papa's happiness was because my schooling would start tomorrow. But seeing Dan Poole smiling, even with missing teeth, made me feel like I could grab a hold of the world and toss it up and catch it.

"Golly," my daddy said. "I ain't breathe so free and easy in more'n twenty year."

"Speak for yourself," Addie panted.

"Scrape us another tune, Dinker," yelled Papa. "I want the whole world to dance all night."

Dancing with my arm around Essie May turn out to be even more fun that I thought. She smiled at me all the time and I felt my face smiling right back at her. Essie sure was pretty and she could step softer than a bug on a leaf. As I holded her hand while we danced, our fingers seem to lace together cozy, and sometime she'd give my hand a little squeeze.

Mrs. Witt sung a song.

Her husband play the fiddle music behind her, as Mrs. Witt sang *Tenting Tonight* in a high fluttery voice. When she sang the last words of the song, "tenting on the old camp ground," people didn't clap right away, because her singing was sweet as a prayer. I notice something else. As Mrs. Witt sang, nobody took a pull from the wine jug. Not even the men folks. Every person in Shack Row sat or stood church quiet as if to bless the words.

Soon as her song got ended, Mr. Witt put

scrawny old arms around his wife to hug her. It was a pleasing sight to see. Nobody could say a word. We just watched and swallowed. Seeing Mr. Witt hug his wife, I knowed, weren't too easy for my daddy. I saw his face harden, guessing that he was probable remembering my mother.

Once the sun sunk, the evening natural turned dark, and the faces of people begun to yawn. So we spruced up our cooking pots and thumped a final push to the wine jug's cork. I don't guess much apple wine was left inside.

"We had a fair time," Papa said. "I hope you had at least half the fun I did, Arly boy."

"Sure did.

One by one, families all turned to go back to their own shacks. All the Cooters went too, leaving me and Dan Poole alone, at our doorway. My daddy looked up at the moon which be no more than a curved sliver off God's fingernail.

"We ought to git ourselves to bed," I said.

"Not just yet," he said, "on account I don't really want our Sunday to end." He sighed. "Lately, it seems like a Sunday only comes along every ten year. Like it never'll come again."

I rested a hand on his shoulder, feeling the rough of his shirt, and the heat left from all his dancing. He felt alive, warm, and I was proud of him. Some people dress fancy on the outside, I was thinking, but somewhere inside Papa there be a fancy that couldn't be store bought. It just prospered there within him, sort of like a sweet-smelling flower that no eye could see, and no ⁓d could pluck away from him.

⁓ morrow."

⁓nly whispered the word, yet I figured I

knowed his thought. Sure enough, I'd reasoned right, because he looked at me with a bent grin.

"Tomorrow," he said, "you start school." His hand cupped my knee. "I ain't never been too strong on thankfulness, but I'm glad. Ya gotta learn, Arly boy. Listen up proper, so you won't be another Dan Poole."

As I held his rough hand, I knowed there was a lot worse things to be.

CHAPTER 8

Monday morning come.

I sure didn't need a peacock to squawk me awake. Papa was up too, and I could tell by the way he run to catch the picker wagon that he'd near be first in line. Not last.

Mr. Roscoe Broda was there, waiting like usual. But I didn't even bother to look his way, nor did Papa. And I was thankful glad he didn't drop his noon bag. One turn at that mishapper was ample plenty. Mrs. Cooter shot me a pie-face grin.

"School's today," she reminded me.

"Yes'm." I winced. "Is Huff going?"

Addie Cooter shifted the mule reins to her other hand. "Hope to tell ya, Arly. All my five's going, unless they want their butts booted or their hides tan."

I waved a so-long to my daddy and scoot back to the shack, ate a stale biscuit, boil me a turnip, and top it off with a cuke. The cucumber I liked the best. Then I left Shack Row and pointed for Jailtown, because I'd promised Papa I'd go, without even a bother to hunt up Huff Cooter. Besides, he'd be going to school with the other four Cooter kids, which ought to full his hands with pester, seeing how Huff was next to eldest.

Essie May Cooter was thirteen, and if'n I dared to do it, I would've walked to school with only her. There weren't hardly a soul in Jailtown who didn't cotton up to Essie May. I sort of figure it out why. Her clothes all pinched a mite too small on her, especially around the chest which looked to me a lot like her mother's. Addie Cooter was no board. Another thing about Essie May was this—the longer her legs growed, seems like the shorter her dresses shrunk up. As to underwear, Essie didn't bother it much.

There was no way, I thought as I headed into Jailtown, that folks would call Essie May Cooter a child. Leastwise, not menfolk who walked behind her and had eyes.

More than one member of the canal dredger crew had took notice of her. The admiration hadn't stopped there. Essie May Cooter's real booster in town was Miss Angel Free who bossed the Lucky Leg. Miss Angel told Essie that whenever the time got ripe for her to look for a job, there was ample work waiting, so Essie told me one time.

When she said it all, I just couldn't make myself believe it, because to picture somebody like Essie May in some fancy dress and all of them ruffles didn't hardly set too good in my mind. Lately, whenever I'd pass by the Lucky Leg Social Palace, it was about all I could reason on, almost seeing Essie inside the place, entertaining the customer men.

Then I recalled how Mrs. Cooter had spoke, earlier this morning, about all her five going to school, and I smiled. Maybe I'd git to sit myself beside Essie May.

I whistled through town.

Mrs. Stout was sweeping off the wood planks outside her store, right next to where the school was going to meet.

39

"Morning, Mrs. Stout."

"Morning." She didn't waste a smile.

"Looks to be a nice day."

Mrs. Stout grunted. "Too early to tell. Maybe it'll be a weather breeder." She leaned on her broom. "I s'pose you're here for the schooling." To me, she didn't sound too happy about having Miss Binnie Hoe next door, in the empty store.

"Yes'm."

Her broom swatted at a big old horsefly. "You pickers is gettin' mighty uppity."

I leaned against a porch post. "Maybe so."

"Huh! No maybe about it. What all you black-soilers need is work. When I be your age, I weren't hangin' round no schoolhouse. Jailtown needs a school-teacher 'bout as much as I need another bellybutton." She took a breath. "Uppity."

"Papa says up is a good direction."

Mrs. Stout pointed the bristle of her broom at me. "Don't you dare sass me none, young Poole. You do, and the wage book'll bring you and your pa back down to soil and sensible."

For some time, I'd notice that Mrs. Stout be one of the people who wore shoes. So around her I'd best mind my manners.

"I'm real sorry, Mrs. Stout. Honest, I sure don't ever mean to sass nobody. Maybe I'm just a bit joyous."

"Joyous? Pickers ain't got no right to joyous." Her fingers bit into my chin, not quite as hard as I figured she wanted them to. "Jailtown don't need no school tax, and it don't need no fancy city female to schoolteach it."

"Yes'm."

"What's going on here?"

As I felt Mrs. Stout's fingers loosen on my face, I

turned to see Miss Binnie Hoe, who was about half of Mrs. Stout. Yet I could see that our lady storekeeper was more than some rattled.

Miss Hoe walked up to her. "If you wish to pinch someone's face, you can start right now and practice on mine."

I saw Mrs. Stout's hands tighten to the broom handle. Maybe she was fixing to give Miss Hoe a hefty swat, and was thinking it all over. Miss Hoe's hands weren't too idle. Her fists doubled up. Mrs. Stout was bigger, by lots, yet Miss Hoe sort of looked to me a bit like a hard little hornet.

Brother Smith come along and took off his hat.

"Good morning, sisters." His deep velvety voice seemed to bless the day. Brother had a way of pouring words on trouble like they was liniment.

Mrs. Stout shot a mean look to Brother Smith and then told him she didn't approve of no darky not knowing his place and speaking first to white ladies. And that she weren't about to be a sister to his kind, or to schoolmarms neither. Turning, she stomped inside her store.

The five Cooter kids arrived, but that was all. Just us seven. I took a chair in the vacant store where I could just sit and look at Essie May Cooter's legs. Standing up, Essie was pretty enough. But in that old chair, her dress just kept shrinking up into wrinkles and her legs twitched to one another like two serpents in love.

Brother Smith sat away in the back, in the biggest chair, folded his big black hands in his lap and listened to every single word Miss Binnie Hoe said, like it was Gospel. I didn't plan to pay it much mind.

Miss Hoe asked us our names. "I already know Brother Smith," she said, "but I would like to learn your names as well." She nodded to Huff's sister.

Essie May didn't say anything. She just stare down at her knees, trying to cover up her thighs with both hands, on account her dress be so short and raggy.

"What's your name, please?"

"Essie."

"That's a beautiful name. And I bet the rest of your name is every bit as pretty."

"Essie May Cooter."

Miss Hoe smiled. "My, I was right. And you?" She looked at Huff.

"Huff Cooter. I'm brother to Ess."

"Yes, I can see you favor each other some."

Jackson Cooter told who he was, and so did Delbert. But little Flo kept quiet.

"Her name's Florence," said Huff.

Miss Hoe asked me who I was. So, just for the smart of it, I said, "My name is Captain Tant."

"Are you really?"

Before I could answer, Brother Smith piped up. "Oh, Missy Hoe, don't pay Arly Poole too much mind."

She looked at me. "Arly, is it?"

Brother smiled. "He one of God's ideas."

CHAPTER 9

"**H**ow many come?" Papa asked.

The two of us stood out behind our shack, near the live oak trees, skinning a catfish. We'd have ourselfs a fair supper, Papa and me. From inside our shack, the smell of boiling collards come from the pot on our cookstove, and we still had a few swallows of vinegar to pour on, once the greens got boiled to a tender. We'd have cucumbers too. Papa had picked cukes today.

"Seven," I told him.

His face frowned. "That ain't right to me. Seems like it ought to be double. Who come?"

"Brother Smith, the five Cooters, and me."

Papa's knife cut a slit under the white throat and he run it down to near the tail. We'd stab a stick through the gills and hung our catfish twixt trees, about eye high. The knife worked in to carve out a fin which Papa tossed to the ants.

"More'll come, boy. This'n here was only the first day, so's you tell Miss Hoe that. She'd get more if'n Brother Smith stayed away." He sighed. "Tell me what you got learned." Papa put a rough thumb to tough catfish skin, and pulled.

"She hung up a map."

"I seen a map once. Long time back."

"Miss Hoe said a map was a picture of land, but it sure don't look like any land I ever saw."

"What land was it?"

"Florida."

Papa yanked on the skin. "That's right here."

"Maybe so, but her map that she tacked up on the empty store wall don't look a whole much like Jailtown, or Shack Row."

"What'd it look like?"

"To me, it looked like a thumb. She made us all say Florida. The first letter is a *F*."

Bending down, I made a *F* in the black earth, but as it didn't pan out so hot, I rubbed it over with my toes, to start pure. On the second try, I did it handsome.

"There," I said. "That's a *F*."

Holding his knife, Papa looked at the letter I'd drawed in the dirt. "Letters look a some like people," he said. "Like ladies and gents with arms and legs. Animals too."

"They's too many letters to learn," I said.

"How many?"

"I think Miss Hoe said twenty-six. Like a quarter and a penny."

"What's a *F* do?"

I smiled at the catfish. "It starts words, like fish."
Papa nodded.

"Fish, flower, and fern. Yes, and a fox. Or family. *F* starts 'em all, Papa. Miss Hoe said. She knows more than spooky. I bet she knows ever letter there is in the whole world."

Papa shook his head. "Ya wonder how some folks git to be so smarty. And then, people like us Pooles."

"Well, she can keep smart. Because I don't be fixing to go to school much."

"How'd old Huff learn up?"

"Not so hot. On the way home, he told me that Miss Hoe was a liar, and that a *F* couldn't draw both a fox and a flower. On account they sure don't look alike to him."

Papa itched his neck. "I don't guess they do, now that you speak it out."

"Florida is bigger than Jailtown. I learned that, too."

"How big is she?"

Thinking real hard, I held up my arms so's they be a same size as our wall map at school. "Florida is this big." It sounded dumb. Maybe I didn't soak it all in today or get the straight of it.

Papa slid his knife blade into his belt, rested both hands on my shoulders, then looked me in the eyes. "Arly, I don't guess you yet know that in school you got to listen up. I don't reason a whole lot, boy, but I bet Florida's got to be bigger than what your two arms can measure."

I nodded. "I figure so." My mind was all mixed up and I couldn't explain the map.

"Boy, this is your one chance. Miss out, and you'll turn out to be nothin', like me." He held my head in his hands. "You got to, Arly. All the stuff Miss Hoe teaches, you got to study smart on and learn. Ever word, ever letter . . ."

I felt his body shake. He was trying so hard to tell me so much, and that he wanted to learn it too, right along with me.

"I'll try, Papa."

He shook his head. "You got to more'n try. I don't want my child booted into no picker's wagon and then stoopin' to cukes all his life. Basket after basket, and day upon day, with nary to collect from the pay ledger, come Saturday night."

As he spoke all the words, I could hear his lungs working. I guessed that cropdust was still ample inside his chest, left over from the years he'd rode the cropduster wagon through the citrus groves, beating the chemical bag with a long pole which clouded the white powder on the trees.

"Education," said Papa, "is a leg up. It's more'n letters, Arly boy. It's a stool to stand taller on. It's a leg up the ladder."

"Maybe so."

"Learning," he said to me, "is what pays to store." His finger tapped my temple. "Right in here. Nobody can never take a cinder of learning away from you, Arly, once you master it and put it by. Nobody, not even the Captain hisself."

"I will."

"Best you do, son."

His hand brushed some dirt off my face. "Learning, boy, is sort of like when you got to move a big load of hefty cement blocks. You don't motion the whole batch of it to once. Only one block to a time. It'll budge hard. Nothin' worth a speck picks up easy. But I tell you true . . . pickin' ain't easy neither. You bend and you sweat them baskets full 'til your whole body nears crying. Saturday last, I worked them cukes on half pay."

"I know, Papa."

"But all the clean day long, I didn't see me them baskets of cucumbers. Ya know what I was seeing?"

"No."

"I seed you, Arly, in school. I could vision all the precious learning that'd feed your head, with ever cuke my hand'd yank off them vines. Monday's what I thought on, all day."

Leaning to me easy, one of his skinny arms hung around my shoulders, and with the other arm he pointed at where we pickers lived. "Shack Row, this place is called. Right now, it's our home. But it ain't the whole world, Arly boy. It ain't no sin to be here. But for you, it'd be a sin to settle for it."

"That's funny," I told him.

"What is?"

"Because that's sort of the same thing Miss Hoe told us. She said to bust out of Jailtown, we'd need ourselfs a ticket. Then she pointed at her own self to say that she was our ticket out of town."

Papa nodded. "Lord bless her."

CHAPTER 10

S"un's going down," said Huff.

I looked out over the tippy-top leaves of the thicket of custard apple trees. "Sure is." It was nice to watch the sun bless the sky, like it was thankful for a good day.

Both of us had eaten supper, so we were wandering toward Jailtown, just to look the place over and check to see if'n any of the drege crew were stirring up sport.

"How'd ya take to school today, Arly?"

"I liked it real good," I lied.

"Well, I sure don't." Huff kicked a pine cone. "It's too hard."

I looked at him with a real even stare. "So's pickin', in case you ain't yet took notice."

He gave me a solid punch. "You don't need tell *me* about pickin', Arly Poole. I picked more'n you. Ask your pa."

"Yeah, that's for true."

"Anytime the roster ain't full, Roscoe Broda comes to our shack to git me'n Essie May. He usual gits *her* if'n the docket'll only fill up with one. And I know why."

Looking at Huff, I felt sort of afraid to ask about

Mr. Roscoe Broda and Essie May Cooter. I'd see Roscoe look to her more'n one time. And it weren't just recent. He'd been turning an eye to her since she was passing by twelve; on account now that Essie was way beyond thirteen, she was tall as Addie, her ma. Also near as womany.

"Does your ma know?"

He nodded his head. "Sure enough do. Ma tells Ess that if'n she sets her cap for him, that she'd be Mrs. Roscoe Broda in a couple years. That'd move us to Easy Street. Roscoe's got a dollar or two, Ma says."

It made me sick to listen it. In my throat, I could taste collards and catfish but mostly vinegar.

"No," I said.

"Huh?"

"Essie May's too nice to marry up Roscoe Broda. I don't want her to."

"Ma does. And then don't because I guess she knows that Roscoe's got a mean streak."

It was my turn to kick a pine cone, so I booted one, and real hard. My toe stubbed on a tree root, which danced me round some while Huff Cooter laughed hisself silly.

"Don't you worry none, Arly. It ain't going to happen right soon."

"Why not?"

"On account Roscoe's got a plan or two about Easy Street for his own self. And it's all got to do with him and Miss Liddy Tant, the way folks tell it. Miss Angel's sweet on him too."

"Yeah, so I hear."

"I don't know much," Huff said, "yet I do know this. Roscoe Broda's a greeder."

"What's that s'pose to mean?"

"A gent, as fancy as Roscoe sees hisself, he'll cotton to have two women. One for bed and one for banking."

I sure knew which was which, I was thinking, wishing righteous awful that I was already a growed-up man. Maybe I'd just have to first pack in the schooling.

"Hey!"

Looking at Huff, I saw that he was watching a guy I'd never seen before. A city man, for sure. He wasn't a dredger, that was certain, nor was he a cane mill worker. But he was a real mess. Clothers were cut to a tatter, and he looked to me that he'd got lost out in the swamp glades, or he'd run through a long ways of sawgrass. His shoes looked rotted wet and near to falling off both his feet.

"I know him," Huff said.

"Who's he be?"

"His name's Mr. Mayland. He's a mapper. You know, he's one of them gents that always gets sent to here to Okeechobee by the government, to make maps of the place. Captain don't like mappers, Ma says, and Broda hates 'em even worse."

Huff and I walked closer to where the man had set hisself down, right near to out front of the harness maker's place. As we got close up, he looked at Huff and me and spoke.

"Howdy."

"Are you Mr. Mayland?" Huff asked him.

"I'm not sure. I been lost out there," he said, pointing at the sundown. "Nobody sane or sober can map this hell hole. I'd settle up my transit on a tripod, like always, but the legs would sink so deep into the swale that it forced me to squat or lie down to sight through it."

"Well," said Huff, "you ain't the first mapper to

quit and leave Jailtown. I seen plenty others, and I don't guess you'll be the last."

"I lost my binoculars and half my stakes. It's crazy out there. The bubble in my level's always off-kilter. I can't true it to take an elevation."

As he talked on, shaking his head, I didn't savvy even the first word of it, but it made a sport to listen. Maybe I'd fetch up some useful learning.

"Okeechobee just runs off places into dead rivers," Mr. Mayland went on saying. "Cricks that don't *go* anywhere, except into marsh and muck, and those places are crawling with cottonmouth snakes, gators, bogs, floating clumps of brush and slime that drift with a current. Trouble is, the dang current's going nowhere."

Mr. Mayland looked up and smiled. Maybe on account both me and Huff Cooter were smiling at his story. He wore a decent look.

"Boys, I've been here in Jailtown almost a week, and your two faces are the only ones who ever looked at me friendly."

He held out his hand and I shook it, just like I was somebody. Huff shook hands with him, too.

"The name's Harry Mayland. I'm a surveyor. Or supposed to be one. Right now, I don't know what I am, except maybe thankful I'm alive. Never did I think I'd be glad to see Jailtown." He looked up and down the road. "Golly, what a dump this place is."

If you think it's ugly *here*, I was thinking, wait until you take yourself a healthy squint at Shack Row.

"Your hand's sort of bloody," I said.

"Want to know how that happened? I somehow walked into a spider web. Never had I seen a spider that size. I could have thrown a saddle on that critter and rode it clear back to Moore Haven."

"It was probable a wolf spider," Huff said. "They sprout up real prosperous around here."

"That web would have covered half the side of a house. And I walked into it, then panic hit me, so I bolted and caught my foot in a tangle of gourd vines and tore my hand on the spines of a fanpalm stem. Some country."

"I bet you learned ample," I said.

"Well, I'm convinced that to survey the total territory around Okeechobee will require a right smart amount of patience, time and misery." Mr. Mayland cracked a palm with a fist. "I met an interesting fellow, though. Calls himself Ed Nocker. He's got one ear and lives in a shack over on one of those dead rivers I was telling you boys about."

"What's he do?" Huff asked.

"He's a squatter. Claims that Roscoe Broda's been attempting to run him out of there for years, but he won't budge. When I met up with Ed, he was skinning down a rattler that was near a foot longer than I am tall. Then he boiled the snake's head to loosen up the fangs."

"Honest?"

Mr. Mayland nodded, reaching in his pocket to pull out a white curved needle. Then a second one. He gave one to me and the other to Huff.

"Here ya go, boys. Ed Nocker says that if you ever want a toothpick that'll last you a lifetime, you can't beat a rattler fang."

"Thanks," I said. Huff thanked him, too. "What else do you learn out in the swampy places?"

"Well," he said, "I learned enough misery to make me wish I'd stayed myself in school longer, and maybe now had me a softer job."

CHAPTER 11

I raised my hand. "I know."

It was another morning in the vacant store that was next to Mrs. Stout's place. Miss Binnie Hoe had just took a white thing and drawed three lines on the board wall and then asked us what it was. She nodded to me and my grin.

"Arly?"

"It's a *F*," I said.

"Very good." Miss Hoe smiled. "Today we're going to try and remember some of the good things, the words, that begin with the letter *F*."

"Fox," I said real quick, "and Florida."

"And," said Miss Hoe, "we will also give *everyone* a chance to recite." She eyed me real steady as she said it and then shifted her look to the back of the store. Turning around, I saw Brother Smith stand up. There was a wide smile on his face.

"Fish," he said. I don't know why we all clapped our hands, but we did, and I could see how joyous it made Brother. He clapped, too. "I can learn," he said. "Can't I, Missy Hoe?"

"Yes, indeed you can." Miss Hoe looked more than just some pleasured. "Now then," she went on, holding up the white thing, "this is chalk. It can draw pictures and also make a letter. Who wants to come forward and draw a great big *F* on the wall?"

Nobody moved. Next to me, I saw one of the two new kids, a dredger's boy, slump down low in his seat, so he'd not git called on by our teacher lady.

Miss Hoe stepped forward, handing the chalk to Essie May Cooter. Essie didn't reach out to take it, not at first, but then she did. She went up to the board wall and stood there in her short dress. Her bare legs sure looked pretty. As she turned around with her back to us, facing the wall, she reached the chalk up real high and her skirt skinned up, too. It covered her sitdown but not much more. She started to draw an *F* and her whole body moved, almost like she was dancing it, instead of just drawing. One of her legs bent a bit into a right beautiful curve.

"That's right," said Miss Hoe. "You made a good line for the trunk of the letter, straight down. Now just add the two arms."

Essie May just stood there, looking at her one big line. Then she chalked the two little lines, to make an *F*. She did the top one first. Making the bottom one, she bent down some, and her own bottom nudged out real handsome.

"That's very good, Essie May," said Miss Hoe.

Huff's sister smiled, handing the chalk thing back to Miss Hoe, and then she come back to take her chair, near mine. There be little spots of white on the ends of her fingers. Somehow, she sensed I was looking at her, real hard. I saw a look in her eyes that I hadn't ever seen before. It made me wonder if Essie ever looked at Mr. Roscoe Broda that same slow way. Maybe it sounds dumb, but Essie May could smile with her whole entire person.

My back started to itch.

"Now," said Miss Hoe, "an *F* all alone does not spell a word. But if we add two more letters, it can help. This letter," she said, using the chalk on the wall, "is an *A*. And this letter is a *T*. See how a *T* looks like a tree?"

She now had something of the board that looked like *FAT*. "Can anyone guess what these three letters now spell? It's a word."

Nobody spoke up.

Looking over at Huff Cooter, I could see that he was near as puzzled as I was. I wanted to guess it was *fish*, but I decided to keep mum and sweat it out.

"It spells *fat*," Miss Hoe told us. "This is an *A* and this is a *T*. Together, they spell *AT*. But when the *F* is in front, it makes *fat*."

I felt ample glad I hadn't said fish.

"Fat," said Brother Smith. "That's right good." As he grinned, his big hand patted his belly.

Miss Hoe drawed a curve. "This," she told us, "is a *C*."

People in Jailtown oft said that Okeechobee used to be a sea, so the sound of it got me a mite mixed up. Besides, the chalk *C* that Miss Hoe made sure weren't blue, like the lake. It was whiter than the inside of a moc-snake's mouth. Like cotton.

"*C - A - T* spells *cat*," said Miss Hoe.

Cats sure don't swim in no sea, I was thinking, and not in no lake. Miss Hoe was going too fast. Brother Smith was scratching his head, like me. I sure didn't figure that school was going to be this thorny.

"This is an *R*," said Miss Hoe. "And now *R - A - T* spells a word. It's a little gray animal with a long tail that sometimes nibbles into our food, late at night, unless we own a cat to catch him. Who knows which animal *R - A - T* spells?"

"Mouse," I said. All the kids clapped, so did Brother Smith, and it made me feel prouder than pie. Essie May looked at me respectful.

"Arly," said Miss Hoe, "that was a very brave answer. And I want you to be pleased that your answer was very close to being correct."

"It was wrong?" As I ask the question, I felt my hands melting.

"Well," she said, "let's just say it was almost right. But I want you to change your answer, Arly. Because if $F - A - T$ is *fat*, and $C - A - T$ is *cat*, then this R sound . . . right here in front, makes . . ."

It hit me! "*Rat*," I told her. "Did I read, Miss Hoe?"

"Yes," she said, in a husky tone. "You can read, Arly Poole."

It was right then that Brother Smith jumped up and come to me, pulling me up and out of my chair, waving me around in the air in circles, and clogging a jig at the same time. It made me dizzy, but it felt precious fine. I don't guess I'd ever felt like I was a famous person or anything any bigger than a picker's kid on Shack Row. But now I was.

I was Arly Poole, a reader.

It took poor Miss Hoe near to all her polish just to work us all quiet again, and back into our chairs. We'd sure made the dust fly in that only empty store, hooting and hollering like we done. Miss Hoe sneezed. At the doorway, I saw Mrs. Stout poke her face in, as if wondering what was going on and was we holding a celebration. Then she just sort of shook her head, real disgustful, looking like she'd up and ate what didn't settle in too sweet. Papa once said he thunk that Mrs. Stout got weaned on a pickle, and it sure put me into a giggle, just thinking about it in school.

"Rat," said Brother Smith. "I can read it, too, Missy Hoe. I can hear a R sound, like the way Arly do."

"Bully for you," Miss Hoe said to Brother. "See how we all gallop ahead? Now, while we're rolling, let's think of another word that might start with an R."

"Rump," said Huff. He stood up and slapped his own backside. "Rump got an R sound. Ain't that right, Miss Hoe?" As he said it there was an edge in his voice, like he wanted to rile her. But I could see that Miss Binnie Hoe got sawed out of tough bark.

"Yes," she told Huff Cooter, "and so does *rude*."

CHAPTER 12

Brother Smith and I stayed after school.

While I busied our old broom to lick out the sand, Brother rag the walls clean. Then he left with Miss Hoe, walking along behind her, holding his big hat. The two of them looked like a tot of a little girl leading a plowhorse.

Brother done the same yesterday.

When school ended, he'd walked several strides behind Miss Binnie Hoe back to Newell's Boarding House, the place where Miss Hoe'd took herself a room. Some of the dredgers boarded there, at Mrs. Newell's. I didn't like the men of the dredger crews a whole ample lot. They'd usual hang around evenings in Jailtown to point their dirty fingers at people and laugh. Yet I had me a happy hunch not a manjack would point too much at Miss Hoe when Brother Smith was nearby. His fists knuckled up bigger than some men's shoes.

Huff's ma told us once that whenever she'd look at Brother Smith's face, she could almost hear a hymn. Addie figured that God sort of looked some like Brother.

There wasn't any church in town. Papa said it was a crime to have no place to worship. So I guess Jailtown was ample lucky to have a man who thought that all men were his brothers.

When I left the vacant store, our school room, I headed home for Shack Row. Then I saw Essie May Cooter talking to Miss Angel Free who was boss of the Lucky Leg. She was all spank out in a red satiny dress. Miss Angel sure could gussy up her person real splendid. She was smiling at Essie, and I guessed I knew why.

Miss Angel took off the fancy bonnet she was wearing to let Essie May try it on her own head. Then she tied a bow beneath Essie's chin. But as far as I could see, the bonnet didn't fit Essie May too proper. The fancy of it didn't fit her face neither. To my way of thinking, Essie May Cooter didn't need a frilly hat to pretty her. In fact, seeing her in Miss Angel Free's bonnet made me notice her ugly for the only time. It was all I could do to keep from running over to where the two of them were standing, untie the bow, then snatch the fancy bonnet off Essie's head. Yet I held myself in rein. To stir trouble with Miss Angel Free would only hatch worse trouble, and Mr. Roscoe Broda might harden the field work on Papa.

Folks in Jailtown usually claimed that Miss Angel was our number-one handsome woman. But right then, as I watched her sweet-talking Essie May, she looked downright piggy, and like she was fixing to throw mud on Essie May's life, and on mine.

If only there be some way to make sure Essie May Cooter never goes to live at the Lucky Leg. The thought of it near to killed me. Essie just weren't intended to be one of those dressed-up ladies with color on her face. Not that I was holding myself up to be better than the fancy women. Just different. Essie was too. People in Jailtown seemed to believe that, sooner or later, Captain Tant would own us all, heart, mind and soul. Maybe they actual didn't *like* believing it, but a passel of them nodded to it, sure as tomorrow.

As I watched, Miss Angel stuck a hand into her beaded purse and pulled out a looking glass.

"See yourself," she told Essie. "You look so pretty natural in my bonnet. Honest do. Why, I declare, people will be coming to town on the boat someday, just to sport a look-see at you, Essie. And I'd wager they'll snap your picture. If I had a camera right now, I'd take your photograph myself."

Miss Angel carried on and on.

So I turned myself away and headed alone for Shack Row, a place where there weren't no fancy ladies or gussy-up clothes. For some reason, the gray boards of Shack Row and the plain of its people was a welcome sight, a lot more comforting than the picture I could remember of Miss Angel's bonnet on Essie's head. Thinking on it turned my hands to fists. Somebody ought to stand up to Roscoe Broda and to Captain Tant.

But, as I recalled about school and Miss Hoe, I sure weren't fixing to ever sass Miss Liddy Tant. No sir. Because the way I figured, it be Miss Liddy who'd done Jailtown a decent turn.

"Thank you, Miss Liddy," I said to the heavens.

There weren't much sense in hanging around Shack Row, and I didn't feel much like looking up Huff Cooter. He'd only badmouth our school. So instead, I took me a stroll toward the big lake. Okeechobee could certain shine in the afternoon, like the sunshine near to polished it into silver. Squinting and shading my eyes with a hand, I looked out across the water to where its edge greeted the sky. Sure was a piece away. It took me to wonder what lay beyond Okeechobee.

"Whatever it be," I said, "it's distant."

In school today, Miss Hoe said that our entire

world was round, like an orange she was holding in her hand. Nobody believed it except me. Because whatever Miss Hoe said, to my thinking, was the Gospel truth. Our teacher also said we didn't have to take her word for it, because all we had to do was level our eyes across Lake Okeechobee and take a look for ourselfs. We'd notice that the lake appeared to be flatter than a board, but it weren't, as there was a curve to it like the outside of her orange.

"Learning," Miss Hoe had told us, "is something like an orange too." On the outside, it weren't too good to taste. Even bitter as a orange rind. But inside, once the learning settles in your head, it becomes sweet. Sweeter than candy.

To prove it, Miss Hoe broke the big orange apart. But first, we had to taste the skin. Then the inside. Huff Cooter had made a face at me, as if to say that Miss Hoe weren't telling anything that he already didn't know. Yet I reasoned real quicksome what she was driving at, and it made a spate of sense.

I spotted a rowing boat.

The boat was heading my way, away off to the left, nosing through the shadows of the overhanging cypress trees, riding low in the water. Two men were aboard. One was rowing. It made me itch to learn who they were and what they were doing. As the boat nosed closer, it was plain to see that the two gents was plume hunters.

Their sculler boat was loaded high with a cargo of dead birds. A lot were white egrets. Some was pink curlews and spoonbills. One orange flamingo. Near the stern, where the man who weren't rowing sat with a pair of shotguns, was a basket of dead parakeets. It weren't a happy sight to see. Alive birds are. Not these.

61

"Boy!" one of the men shouted to me. "What be the name of this here sorrowful place?"

"Jailtown," I said.

The man who'd spoke at me was bigger than the rowing man. He was smaller and leaner. The big man who was sitting the stern spat a brown stream of tobacco juice into the lake, just before I heard the prow of their rowboat grind her nose into the shore sand, then rock to a rest.

"Yeah," the man said, "this here's the right town."

"How come you got to shoot so many of them pretty birds?" I asked.

Squinting at me like I was three kinds of fool, the big man answered. "Hats," he said. "Ladies who dress up real fancy, in city places, wear all them birdie feathers on a hat." He spat again. "But it ain't no business of yours."

"No," I said, "I don't guess it is. But maybe it's sort of a shame all them little birds got to get gunned."

The small man spoke up. "You're right, son."

"Shut up, Joshua," the big gent spoke. "Besides, I took me a notice of how you're usual eager to pocket the money."

In turn, the two plume hunters climbed out of their sculler. As they done so, their heavy boots stepped on the pile of birds. Even though they were all dead, it was more than hurtful to watch.

"You want to earn a dime, boy?"

I nodded.

"There a livery stable in town?"

"Yes."

The big man flipped me a dime, but I dropped it. Bending over to fetch it from the mud, I heard the bigger gent laughing at me.

"You hightail yourself to the livery stable and git

somebody to snake back here pronto with a mule and a buckboard wagon. Hear? It's still light enough to go back into them dead rivers and kill us another load."

Inside my hand, I could feel the dime. And it would do handy. But I couldn't make my feet go. If I fetched the wagon in a hurry, maybe a lot more birds would die.

"Git going!" the big man yelled.

The edges of his dime was biting into my hand, because I was squeezing it so hard and wanting it even harder.

I tossed him the dime and ran.

CHAPTER 13

I couldn't eat.

All I could do was keep seeing that boatload of dead color, all them little silent birds. So I boiled some cabbage for Papa and made up a story, a lie, saying I'd already ate before he'd climbed off the picker wagon.

"I'm wore out, Arly," he said, then folded down to his tick and sound like he was instant asleep. His breathing wheezed in and out.

After soaping his plate and our cookpot, I went outside our shack, around back where the sand was soft, to scratch a few letters in the dirt. I made all the letters that Miss Hoe learn us. Ever single one, and did them over and over, spelling the little words. Most words come right easy on account there be only three letters inside each one. Shack was a leadpipe cinch to spell.

S - H - C.

Yet as I studied the letters I'd fingered into the sand, the word didn't look right, on account I'd forgot to place a *A* in it. Words usual had a *A* in the middle, like *rat* and *cat* and *hat*. I sighed. Education sure could be thorny. In school, being wrong had a way of cutting my brain, the like way a stem of a fan palm could cut a hand. It was hurtsome. But the bleeding was all inside me where only I could feel the misery of it.

Even though I was staring down at my letters I'd drawed in the dirt, my mind kept on seeing the dead birds.

It was near dark, and evenings were usual a happy time for me, because Papa was resting in shade and not stooping in the heat to endless rows of vegetables. But I couldn't turn myself too joyous. It wouldn't be right to allow a happy feeling on a day when so many of God's ideas all got scatter-gunned into a pile of feathery death. Just for hats.

"Arly?"

It weren't necessary for me to look up to learn who'd spoke my name. Her voice I already knowed like it was near a song. But I did look up to see her.

Essie May Cooter come strolling my way, wearing her skimpy dress in a manner like she wanted to wish it bigger, as if she feared everybody in jailtown was looking at her, and laughing. Or thinking worse. She stood sort of hiding inside her dress.

"Howdy," I said.

"Sure is hot. What you doing out here?"

"Practicing my letters, the way Miss Hoe said we probable ought, so's we would remember."

Essie leaned against the trunk of a custard apple, looking up at the still-light sky, hauling in a deep breath and then letting it loose really slow. "I talked to Miss Angel today. She let me try on her bonnet."

That I knowed, because I'd seen it all happen. But no words about it would come out my mouth. All I done was kick at the letters with my toes until every word I'd wrote got destroyed.

"In our shack," Essie said, "I can't seem to breathe no longer. There's only your pa and you in your place, but us Cooters got six. Ain't even room to turn over, on account if I do in the night, I'll wake up little Florence and she'll wail. Soon, I got to have me a room of my own."

"Is that what Miss Angel promised you?"

Essie May nodded.

Seeing her do such was so hurtful I couldn't hardly abide it. Yet I was afraid to run away, recalling the night a picker runned off. Before sunup, Roscoe Broda and some other men on horses had rope-dragged Mr. Yurman all the way back to Shack Row. He was nothing but earth and blood. And then, as if'n that weren't enough punishing, Clete Yurman sweated a week on no wages. Broda had even worked him on a Sunday.

"I can't live in Shack Row no longer," Essie said. "A body can't stand to stay where there ain't enough space. Huff's fixing to scamper off some night."

I looked at her. "He say so?"

"Not actual. He knows they posted guards down the road. Jailer Jim Tinner's men, carrying guns, and with tracker hounds. Huff claims he can swim across the lake."

"He'll drown. Ain't nobody about to swim across Okeechobee. All he'll be is gator meat."

Essie May nodded. "Huff says it'd be better to die free than live a whole life in Jailtown. All I know is, Huff fixes to go his way, and I'm near ready to go mine. And I reckon my only chance is . . ."

She couldn't seem to say *Lucky Leg*. All she done was turn about and hug the trunk of the custard apple tree. "I been a mother to Jackson and Delbert seems like forever. And little Flo about thinks I *am* her ma. I love her dear. But sometimes I know I can't stay in our shack no longer. It's like I'm counting days. I told it all to Miss Angel and she understands."

Standing up, I walked quick to Essie, and rested my hand light on her shoulder. But instead of stretching up on my toes, to be as tall as Essie May, I just stood up straight, to be honest. "We got a school now," I said. "We can learn stuff. Miss Hoe says she's our ticket out of Jailtown."

"It's too late, Arly. Maybe not for you, but for Huff and me. The teacher didn't come soon enough. I ain't a child no more. I'm a woman. Miss Angel Free told me so, but I already knowed it. For most of a year."

"You can't, Essie. I won't let you."

Her hands clawed at the bark as if she was trying to climb the tree. "Can't you see it's the only road I got. For me, it'll be either the Lucky Leg or Shack Row. And it sure ain't going to be here. You claim Huff'll drown in the lake. Maybe so. But I'm already choking in our shack . . . us Cooters sleeping like fingers. Well, I ain't a finger much longer. At the Lucky Leg, I can salt away money, and maybe Florence won't have to . . . social dredgers."

Essie May pulled a twig off the tree and was ripping its leaves away, one by each, until no pretty green leaves was left. All of them scattered all twisted and tore at our feet, like a flock of little green birds that once could fly, but wouldn't fly no longer.

Bending, I picked up one of the leaves, trying to smooth it right again, back to how it used to look, fresh and green.

"This ain't the right way for you to end up," I told Essie. "They got a fancy front door at the Lucky Leg. But there's no back door."

She give me a empty look.

"What I mean is this, Ess. It's simple easy to parade inside. Maybe dress fancy. But beyond that, there ain't

67

no escaping. You'll never come out that door again. Papa said that one time, like the Lucky Leg was just another Shack Row, only dressed up."

Essie touched my hand. "Stay to school, Arly."

"How come you're saying that to me?"

"Because you can learn fast," Essie said. "Maybe you're the only one who'll do it. I can't do it. Neither can Huff. You can master it sudden, all of it, all them letters and words and chalk writing. And I hope you do it proper. You'll be doing it for me, and for Huff, and for all the others who won't never get no ticket."

As she said it, I felt myself shaking all over, something like a run-over cat. Like I was dead but still clawing and screeching.

Essie's fingers tightened on my hand. "Thank you for your feelings. I got 'em too. But they be feelings I can't afford to save." Reaching up, she pulled a fresh leaf from a twig, laying beside my tattery one. "You're a whole new leaf, Arly Poole. Me, I'm this used one. I've growed all I can go."

"No," I said. "You're a leaf too. You can learn."

Essie nodded. "I already have. Before I got Miss Binnie Hoe for a teacher, I had me another kind of teacher. I had Mr. Roscoe Broda."

I couldn't speak.

"You mustn't tell nobody," she said. "Mama don't know about it. You're the only person who knows. I just had to tell somebody, and I certain couldn't tell Mama. If she knew, she'd cuss out to Roscoe and git beaten up for her trouble. So I be trusting you, Arly, on account you best know my secret. You're the only friend I got."

"Essie . . . Essie . . ."

We stood behind the shacks alone, sort of holding

on to each other, like nobody was leaving Jailtown, yet we were possible saying good-bye.

"I'll kill Roscoe," I said.

She pulled away from me. "No, you can't. Even if you could do it, it'd be Judge Tinner's chain gang for the rest of your time. He won't hang you, Arly. Nobody dead can work roads. But you'll be worse'n dead, because the jailbirds will do worse to you than Roscoe Broda done on me."

"I got to save you, Essie."

She shook her head. "It's too late. But there be somebody in Jailtown that you could save, if you study on it for a time."

I couldn't think. "Who's that?"

"You."

Essie lightly kissed my cheek and then turned to walk away, as if she wanted to be by her lonesome. Watching her go, I didn't see the Essie May Cooter that I'd knowed all my life.

I saw a dead bird.

CHAPTER 14

It was dark.

Inside the parlor at Newell's Boarding House, a light was burning, and a few of the boarders were chatting away. I was pleased that Miss Hoe was out front, on the porch, sitting in one of those fancy wicker chairs that rocked when you worked it. She sat alone.

"Miss Hoe?"

As I trot up the front walk to the porch stairs, I fretted a mite, about that maybe I'd forgot to know my place. Pickers and colored folks weren't allowed at places such as Newell's Boarding House. But I feel some better when Miss Hoe shade her eyes with her hand, to make out who I was.

"It's me," I told her. "Arly Poole."

"My," she said, getting up from her rocker chair, "what a surprise. How nice to have my very first visitor."

I didn't know quite what to do, yet wanting to do it proper, so I just stood there and wiggled my toes. Then I give her my rattlesnake fang, for a present. "It's for picking your teeth," I said.

"Come," she said, "and sit with me. And thank you for bringing me such a thoughtful gift."

It sure was the shock of my life when I sat myself down in the rocker chair, because it swayed back, and I guess I thought it was fixing to keel me over backwards. My mouth popped open.

Miss Hoe smiled.

"I never sit a fancy chair like this before."

"Then," she said, "it's about time."

"Boy, I sure would like to buy Papa a chair like this, to rest on."

I had stuff to tell her, yet I just sat there, real cautious, so the rocker wouldn't buck me off, and couldn't come out with even my starting word. So I just watched the moth bugs flitter around the porch lamp.

"Goodness," she said, "it certain is welcome to have a nice young man pay a call on his teacher."

"Yes'm."

"Do you live nearby?"

"Pretty close. Over to Shack Row. Me and my daddy, Dan Poole, live lonesome on account Mama died after I got born, years back."

"I'm sorry, Arly."

"Yes'm. I am too. Papa misses her a lot."

"Does your father work in the cane mill?"

I shook my head. "No, he's a picker. Only us pickers live in Shack Row because that's where Captain and Mr. Broda says we do."

"I see. Have you had your supper?"

"Oh yes'm, I sure have," I lied. "Mr. Witt . . . he's a picker too . . . kilt an otter, so he give us some scrappy meat for the beans." I looked at Miss Hoe and smiled. "I ate me some ice cream once."

"I bet you liked it."

"Sure did. It was all pinky and they said it was the strawberry kind. I ate it righteous slow so's it would last. And good? It was like eating flowers."

Miss Hoe looked at me. "You're a bright boy, Arly."

"Me?"

"Indeed you are. I have logged plenty of time, my dear, as a teacher. Years and years. And I can read intelligence."

"I'm just a picker's kid."

"For now, perhaps. But recently I realized that you truly are one of God's ideas."

"Brother Smith said that about me an' Huff."

Miss Hoe nodded. "I have a feeling that you believe the things that Brother Smith tells you. And I bet they're good things to hear."

"Yes'm, they usual are. But I saw trouble today," I burped out, sort of glad I'd got up the gumption to speak mind, and tell Miss Hoe why I had to talk to her, in private.

"Trouble?"

"It's about Essie May Cooter."

Miss Hoe quit her smile. "She's a sweet child, Arly, but I guess you already are aware of that."

"That's why I come to see you."

"Tell me all about it, please."

"Essie ain't a child no longer, Miss Hoe. She's a woman now. And knows so. Some of the menfolk in Jailtown see it too."

I saw my teacher lock her fingers together.

"Essie got a problem, Miss Hoe. Ya see, there's six Cooters to one shack and Essie May can't breathe. My daddy can't breathe good neither, but with Papa it's his lungs, from cropdust. It's different with Essie. Ain't her lungs. The woman inside her is screaming."

Everything I was saying sounded so dumb. I understood it. Yet I didn't guess I'd ever git my teacher to learn it all. Well, I decided, best I just plain open up and spew it all out.

"It ain't polite," I said, "to talk about Miss Angel Free to a lady like you. Even if'n it be poorly to do, I got to git it spoke, straight out."

"Who is Miss Angel Free?"

"Oh, she's the lady who's the boss at the Lucky Leg."

Miss Hoe nodded. "I've noticed the leg. One could hardly miss seeing *that*. Now let me help you out, if I can. Miss Free is interested in Essie May Cooter and perhaps has promised her that she can leave Shack Row and take residence in the Lucky Leg. Is that what worries you?"

"Wow, you sure are smart."

"Thank you, Arly. It's always rewarding when a pupil admits that his teacher is worldly."

"Golly, I didn't mean thataway."

She patted my hand. "I know. Enough about you and me. What's important is Essie May Cooter. Believe me, Arly, in every school I've taught in, there are always young girls who suddenly blossom to womanhood. I see it before they do, usually."

"I look at her too. All the time."

"So I have observed."

"You have?" My palms began to sweat a mite, so I rubbed my hands back and forth on the wicker arms of the chair.

"We old schoolmarms have not lived all of our lives with only a cat for company."

"Yes'm, I s'pose not."

"You're a sensitive young man."

"What does *sensitive* mean?"

She smiled. "It means that you are mindful of the plight of others. In this instance, you're aware of the growing urgings of Essie May Cooter, and you have

Property Pleasant Twp.
High School Media Center 73

even foreseen a possible tragedy that could befall a girl who is now a woman."

"Essie's ma is just a picker too. Addie Cooter. She drives the picker wagon and looks to the mules."

"Perhaps I should meet Mrs. Cooter."

"What we do," I said, "has got to be sudden soon. I'm afraid something bad'll git to Essie May. Each day gits worse an' worse."

I heared a funny sound. It came from inside the house. Bong! Bong! Bong! The noise made me jumpy. "What's *that?*"

"Oh, that's only Mrs. Newell's big grandfather clock. She showed it to me on Sunday and talked about that clock as if it were her prize possession. It just struck the hour. Eight o'clock."

"I don't understand time," I said, "or clocks neither."

"Then you and your father don't own a clock? Even so, you manage to come to school on time."

"Yes'm. I git Papa up righteous early, on account pickers got to be in the fields at first light, to harvest fresh. While he washes, I sort of stuff his noon bag, so's he'll eat proper."

"You care about your father, don't you?"

I nodded. "He's all I got, except for Brother and the Cooters. And you."

"Thank you, Arly. I'm honored that you include me among your friends."

CHAPTER 15

A cheer sounded.

  Jumping up from the rocking chair on the front porch of the boarding house, I looked down the street.

  "Miss Hoe, there's something going on down yonder. A crowd of men are standing around a big crate."

  "Perhaps we should stroll down there and see for ourselves," she answered. "I wouldn't want to miss all the excitement."

  Turning around quickly, I shook my head at her. "No, a lady like you can't go there. Not to a place like that."

  Miss Hoe stood very straight, even though she was a little woman. "Arly," she told me, "a *lady* can go anywhere and still remain a lady." She smiled softly. "Let's go."

  Sure enough, Miss Binnie Hoe walked out of the front gate, made a sharp turn, and pointed herself head-on toward the Lucky Leg Social Palace. Her pace weren't fast. Just steady. As we got closer, we could see a large wooden carton being pried open by two men who were using iron wrecking bars. Pulling nails out of the boards made a high-pitch squeaky sound.

  "What's inside?" I asked.

"Well," said Miss Hoe, "from the rumors I hear from some of the gentleman boarders at Mrs. Newell's, my guess would be that this is a new billiard table."

"A pool table?"

She nodded. "My father built himself one, years ago. He was an excellent billiard shot who, believe it or not, taught me a trick or two."

As it turned out, Miss Hoe was right. There it stood, a beauty of a new pool table with a bright green felt for a playing surface. The men also unpacked balls, cues of different lengths, and some other stuff. Sitting up on the Lucky Leg's porch in her extra-big white wicker chair was Miss Angel Free herself, wearing a fancy dress of white lace, white shoes with pink pointy toes. The pink matched the color of her fingernails and her dangle-down earrings.

"Miss Angel," one of the dredgers said, "maybe you'd ought to step down here, and pocket the first shot."

Moving as slowly as the Caloosahatchee Queen, the bosslady rose from her fancy chair, fanned herself, and then paraded down the steps with a smooth rolling of her ample hips that caught the eye of every nearby gent.

"My," she said, eyeing all the colorful stuff on the table, "I don't guess I was fixing to handle pool balls."

All the men roared. Some clapped.

"Go ahead," said another gent, "try 'er out for size, Miss Angel."

She winked at the man. "All right," she said quietly, selecting a brown cue stick which she fondle with ease, "reckon I just might do such. Seeing as you gentlemen already know that I'm the hottest pool shark in town."

Right then, I got the biggest shock of my whole life. Even though I saw it, and heard it, my brain just wouldn't believe what happened next. Stepping forward and walking to where the pool table stood on the dirt of the street, Miss Hoe picked up a cue stick, smiled at Miss Angel Free, and said two words.

"Second hottest."

A wave of laughter come from the sports who were standing there watching.

"Well," said Miss Angel, "don't tell me that our new schoolmistress is as gifted a pool player as she is around a spelling bee."

"Miss Free," said my teacher, "there's only one way to find out."

Standing there, I couldn't breathe. Only blink. There stood little Miss Binnie Hoe in her plain gray dress, right beside Miss Angel. They looked like a poor mouse and a rich milkcow.

"Charlie," said Miss Angel to one of the toughs, "would you please do us ladies a favor and rack the balls?"

In a breath or two, the fellow named Charlie had all fifteen balls tight-racked and ready for play. Pool was a game I'd never tried. But, aplenty of times, Huff Cooter and I had peeked in the Lucky Leg's parlor window, just to watch, and we'd picked up a word or two of the lingo.

Miss Free won the lag and so it was her honor to shoot the break shot.

"What'll we play?" she asked my teacher. "Do you fancy straight pool? Your choice."

"Eightball," said Miss Hoe.

Miss Angel lifted her chin with a dash of pride. "Good. Eightball happens to be what I'm best at."

"Second best at," one of the sporty gents hollered out, and the rest of the guys laugh to beat all.

Charlie reset the balls for Eightball, placing the

black one in the forward center, and the table was ready. Drawing back her cue, Miss Angel slammed a break shot to scatter the balls like a covey of flushed quail. A yellow ball dropped. The one ball.

"I got the solids," said Miss Angel, meaning the solid-colored low number balls, one through seven. "You take stripes."

"Nifty," said Miss Hoe, "because, for me, those big ringers always seem to drop easier."

Miss Angel sunk a six ball. Then a four. But she missed on the three and muttered a salty word. It was a word I didn't want my teacher to hear. If'n she heard it, she didn't at all let on. Instead, she sunk a long twelve ball, a short ten, banked the green-striped fourteen. Then missed. Miss Angel missed too. Her three ball clogged a corner pocket but wouldn't drop.

"That's fine by me," she said. "It'll block that pocket as long as I desire it to."

Miss Hoe shot a tidy combination shot, the thirteen into the fifteen. Then missed. Miss Angel ran two balls but that was it. Now the white cue ball was froze to a rail, nowhere near any of the stripers, nine through fifteen.

With a smirk on her face, Miss Angel nodded at the cue ball. "I don't guess I left you much."

Bending down low, Miss Hoe sighted up the table. "Enough," she said, and double-banked a long ball, twice across.

"That," said a man, "was a dilly."

However, she missed her next shot. Somebody sneezed during her forward stroke and the cue ball met the ringer too fat. The striper rounded the corner and come to rest at center table.

During the game, the rowdies who stood around were quiet for a change, like they's all watching a prayer.

It was easy to figure that Miss Angel Free had emptied their pockets at the old pool table, inside, so maybe some of the gents were rooting for the schoolmarm. However, when either lady score a difficult ball, like a long shot with a lot of green, or cut a thin shot into a side pocket, the men would clap.

Other than the white cue ball, there were now only three object balls left on the table. A red five ball for Miss Angel to sink, Miss Hoe's orange thirteen and the last ball to drop for either player . . . the black eight.

Miss Angel smiled and chalked her cue.

"My dear Miss Binnie," she said, "would you be opposed to placing a modest wager on the outcome of this game, just to make the event more . . . interesting."

"Miss Free, I'm not a gambling woman. Leastwise, not until I got up the gumption to come to Jailtown. Besides, what little capital I have will be due to Mrs. Newell, for my room at the boarding house."

"Doesn't have to be money. A wager can pit one value against another, deed for a deed. Are you game?"

My teacher nodded. "I'm game. What's your bet?"

"If *you* win," said Miss Angel Free, "I'll donate a book to that empty-store schoolhouse of yours. A book by Mr. Mark Twain himself."

"Done," said Miss Hoe. "And if *you* win, Miss Free, I shall bring clean rags, soap, and a bucket, and I shall personally wash those two large windows in the front of your charming residence." She nodded at the Lucky Leg Social Palace.

The two ladies shook hands.

It was Miss Angel's turn. She missed her shot on the red five by an eyelash. The ball merely hung to the lip of the pocket, yet it didn't fall.

Miss Hoe's shot was a toughie. The cue ball was rail tight, and her orange-striped thirteen was away down at the table's far end. The crowd held its breathing. So did I. Drawing back her cue, Miss Hoe stroke a hard shot. A beauty! The cue ball cut the thirteen into the corner, and then kept rolling, quite fast. Back it bounced, hit the black eight, and the near corner pocket gulped it down.

Miss Hoe lost.

That's what happens when you sink the eight ball by mistake. It had to be a called shot. Yet her shot on the thirteen had been a miracle. A home run.

"You win," said Miss Hoe. "I'll wash those two windows."

"It was still a nifty," said Miss Angel.

CHAPTER 16

We left the Lucky Leg.

Yet not before Miss Binnie Hoe shook hands with a few of the dredgers, and told them their kids would be welcome at the school.

"Arly," she said, "it's still early."

"Yes'm."

"Lately I don't retire as promptly as I used to, so let's take ourselves a stroll, you and I."

"If you want."

Then I up and asked her if there be any one place she'd be fixing to visit.

"Well," she answered, "seeing as you're offering me a choice, I shall make one." She looked smack at me. "I should like to see Shack Row."

I stopped. "No," I said, "you won't cotton it much."

"Perhaps you'll allow me to judge for myself."

"But it's where *pickers* live, Miss Hoe. People like me, and Papa . . . and the Cooters."

"You're not a picker yet, Arly Poole." Miss Hoe stared me right in the eyes. "And if Binnie Hoe is as capable a teacher as I'm convinced she is, you may not *ever* be one."

"Honest?"

"Cross my heart and hope to teach. Which way to Shack Row? Is it far?"

"Not very."

Stopping, I bended myself over, to blow my nose into the dirt. But then, as I straighted up again, Miss Hoe looked at me in a strange way, like I'd done something wrong.

"You don't have a handkerchief?"

I give her a grin. "No, not me. Papa says that a poor man blows his snot on the ground, but a rich man puts it all back in his pocket."

Miss Hoe shook her head, like she couldn't think of anything to say. And I was sort of decided that schoolteachers sure git some odd notions. We walked along together. Seeing as Huff Cooter and I used every single shortcut in Jailtown, along with the fact that Shack Row was only as far as the edge of town, Miss Hoe and me got there sudden quick.

"Which house is yours?"

"Over there. But I don't guess Papa's got an eye for company coming. Dan Poole might be in his underwear. Or worse."

Miss Hoe stiffen her spine. "In that case, Arly, I am sure we will first knock before entering. We'll send you in first. I can't admit that I'd favor your father's calling on me when I was in *my* underwear, so surely we can afford him some preparation."

I laughed right out. "Miss Hoe, you surely got a wit to you. You certain do."

"A teacher with no wit, young man, wouldn't last too long this side of the insane asylum. Now scoot, and tell Mr. Dan Poole that he has a caller."

I bolted ahead and into our shack. Papa was there,

sitting in the dark like usual, down on his tick on the floor.

"Papa," I said, "we got company."

Fading light from a crack in the cookstove lit up his face so I could read his surprise. He jumped up to his feet. I'd been right when I'd warned my teacher that he'd be in his dirty old underwear.

"Here," I said, "pull on your pants."

"Who's coming?" he asked me, stuffing in one skinny leg and then the other. "Tell me it ain't Broda."

"It's Miss Hoe."

"The *teacher*?" As he said it, his fingers let loose of his garment and his pants fell to around his ankles. I helped him fix decent, but then I smelled his breath, which was foul on moon whiskey.

"Papa, you best rinse out your mouth with vinegar, or hold back breathing." I wasn't mad with him. Nobody'd fault a picker from a swig or two of moon after a day of toting cuke baskets to a wagon. Besides, he never oft got what you'd call shirttail drunk. The word he used on himself was *meller*.

He gargled a mouthful of vinegar, spat it to the dirt floor, and turned back to me.

"Reckon I'll do."

"Okay," I said, "because we sure ain't fixing to keep a lady like Miss Hoe waiting outside in the bugs and chizzywinks." I went back out the door and called to her. "Miss Hoe?"

It was dark in Shack Row. So I took her by the hand and into our shack where I struck a match to light the table candle. Slowly I saw its flicker begin to yellow up her smile.

"Mr. Poole?"

"Yes'm," he said. He bent a bow, and to watch him pull it off so proper made me feel righteous proud.

There always had been, I had noticed, a *gent* inside my daddy, as if he'd almost could have been somebody. At the small table in the corner, where we ate, sat a pair of three-leg stools, one of which I dusted off quick with my sleeve, to offer to Miss Hoe. She sat, looking stiff and more than a meager away from home.

"Dan," she said, "you can call me Binnie."

"Oh, *no*," Papa said real quick. "I don't guess I could ever do such, Miss Hoe. Wouldn't be proper to speak to a genuine schoolteacher by her Christian name."

"As you prefer, Mr. Poole. We shall remain formal. However, I am anxious to tell you, sir, how pleased I am that you allow your Arly to be my pupil."

I near to fell over. She'd called Papa *sir*. Nobody ever done that for him. Never. And him just a picker. There sure were a lot to Miss Hoe that I didn't reason out. As she talked to him, I figured something real crazy . . . and it was that if'n Miss Hoe ever talked to Captain Tant, she'd speak just like she be conversating with Dan Poole, or me.

"Thank you, teacher," said Papa. "You know, me an' Arly don't get visitors here to the shack. Leastwise, not famous ones."

"I gather that these houses here belong to Mr. Tant. Is that correct?"

"Yes indeedy," Papa told her. "Truly be. Captain, he own mostly everthing in the whole world. Even me."

"Perhaps," said Miss Hoe, "and then perhaps not. I won't stay long, Mr. Poole, because I do have to trot back to Mrs. Newell's and get my rest. Yet I did want to meet you, sir, and report to you how bright a boy you've raised."

It's hard to strut when you're seated to a low threelegger, but I near to did it. Miss Hoe sure knowed how to dance somebody's heart, namely mine.

Papa took a step to me and rested his skinny arm around my shoulder. "Arly's the salt of the earth. If'n anything ever happened to him it'd rip the sun from my sky. He's all I got. And because they's so much inside him, I reckon I'm a rich man, in ways."

"Mr. Poole, your son can learn to read."

Papa give my shoulder a pat. "You know what, Miss Hoe? Arly says he can teacher me, so's maybe I can just swagger myself over into Jailtown some Saturday night, and buy the weekly."

"Sure you can Papa. Real soon."

"Yessir, I aim to plunk down my two cents, pick up my newspaper, and then sit right prominent on the town bench, and read it." Papa turned complete around, waving his hands, like he was in a jig. "Wouldn't that be grand, Miss Hoe?"

Her voice answered him very quiet. "Yes, it would, Mr. Poole. Very grand indeed."

"I'm glad you come to Jailtown, Miss Binnie Hoe. Sorry, I just got worked up. But I'm sure grateful you come to do teachering."

Miss Hoe stood up. "So am I."

CHAPTER 17

Papa woke me.

"Listen to her, Arly. It's so nifty to harken to a morning mockingbird. I don't guess I'd ever want to live nowhere there weren't no mockingbirds to welcome a morn."

The straw inside my tick whispered as I rolled off it, up and onto my bare feet. The dirt felt coldsome and damp.

"Mules'll be coming soon," I heard Papa say. "I s'pose Addie's already gone to fetch 'em. She'll be back sudden." He rattled the shaker on our little cookstove. Then we fixed what we could locate, some stale biscuits, and boiled three or four handfuls of oatmeal. There was only a few grains of brown sugar left, so I give it all to Papa, on his oats.

We heard the mockingbird again.

My daddy smiled at me. "My," he said, "that there old bird know so many callings. One after another. He's just like you, Arly boy. Inside you, there's a ample lot of songs. Not just a picker song. You got a whole band concert. I'm hoping you'll learn to warble ever one."

A mule brayed.

"Best I git myself aboard," he said.

Still chewing, we both run up the Shack Row road to greet the mules. The wagon weren't there yet. It was a rare morning when Addie Cooter weren't on time and waiting to load on pickers. As we stood in the gray light, the sun nudged awake, and our long shadows got born on the dirt.

Roscoe Broda come cantering on his bay horse. Nobody spoke to him or to anyone else. When he looked at people, they'd just stare down to ground, afraid to heft up their eyes. But not me. I always traded Roscoe look for look. Maybe that be the reason he reined his horse too close to me that morning and made me step back.

"You," he said to me. "Dan Poole's kid . . ." He hadn't talked up to me much before, and never in a friendly way. So I was took back by it. "We're short-handed on the sugar docket. So you march yourself over to the cane mill, boy, and see Lem Rathaway, hear?"

"I got school," I said.

Roscoe spun his horse around, kicking spurs to him. He crowded closer this time. "No you ain't, sassy boy. You an' Addie's lad report to the cane mill."

I saw the look on Papa's face. "No," he said to me in a husky voice. "I don't mean ya to go, Arly. You got to take your schooling."

"Dan Poole, you got some words to say, you best shout 'em right out heavy so's I can hear 'em all," Roscoe Broda said.

Papa blinked. "My boy's got school today. Don't make him work no sugar mill, Mr. Broda. Please let him go to school."

"Don't matter to me if'n his funeral's today," Mr. Broda said. His gelding danced around ample, and I was thinking that even his animal feared him more than some. The horse was sweaty and wild-eyed. "Tell your skinny brat to git over and check in with Lem. Him and young Cooter." He pointed his horsewhip at my face. "And you git a move on, pronto."

"Please." Papa took off his hat. "I'll work double today. I can pick for two, Mr. Broda, to free up an extra hand. I can even work through the noon and not eat nothing."

"Dan, you don't even work single no more. *You* work double? Why, you ain't got the lungs or the legs to sift bug turds out of pepper. Old man, you don't got a thing left. You're lucky that Captain affords you a fancy shack to sleep in and don't charge you hardly no rent."

I wanted to call Roscoe Broda a liar but couldn't, because I didn't know how much rent we paid. Nobody did, because Mrs. Stout took our rent out of Papa's week wages, on Saturday nights.

"Both you Pooles had best mind your manners, because if'n ya don't, maybe you won't have no place in Shack Row. I got new workers signed in soon."

The thought of losing our shack, even if I hated the stink of the place, feared me. I turned wet all over. It'd be a sorry time for Papa and for me if we had no shack. And no wage money to eat on.

"I'll go," I told Mr. Broda.

"See to it then. And take the Cooter bum along and report. Move."

I left, went back to our shack, and tried to eat. But the cold biscuit tasted too dry to choke down, like I was efforting to gnaw dust. Swallows of pump water didn't help. Leaving our place, I trotted down Shack Row to where the five Cooters would be brushing up for school. Essie was braiding little Florence's hair into pigtails and had her decked out in a clean dress. They both sat on their front stoop.

"Essie, where's Huff?"

"Inside."

"Huff," I hollered, "you an' me can't go to the school today."

I saw the surprise on Essie May's face as Huff came to the door. "How come?" he asked me.

"Roscoe Broda said. They's shorthanded at the sugar mill, so you an' me gotta git there and report to Mr. Lem Rathaway. And sudden."

Huff sighed. Work never had hurried him a whole lot. He spat into the sandspurs. "Essie May," he said to his sister, "I guess you gotta take the little ones to the school place."

"It ain't fair," she said.

If'n you was a picker, or a picker's kid, you best go where you git ordered. It was like we was ants. I'd watched a anthill one time, and they didn't seem to do any deciding on their lonesome. They just sort of did, and done and kept on doing . . . like there was no right or wrong to it. And that's what a picker in Shack Row was, nothing but a little ant, working and waiting for the boot of somebody like Roscoe Broda to stomp on your hill.

"Be careful," Essie May told Huff and me.

Bending down, Huff kissed little Flo. Her smile was prettier than a weed flower. I never seen Huff Cooter do a thing like that before. Usual, he was the bully of the family. There was some dirt on Florence's hand, so he pulled a rag out of his pocket, twisted it to a white spot and wiped his tiny sister. No angel could've done the job more gentle.

"Come on, Arly," he said.

We headed for the sugar mill that was set back from the water edge of Okeechobee. In a way, I felt glad to be a wager, and earn to help Papa.

Our day with Mr. Rathaway never seemed to come end. First he had us chopping down cane, by hand, then stacking it into a one-mule wagon. We hauled it to the crusher and helped feed it into where it'd become pulp. The work was a sour business, but the cane smell at the crusher was sweeter than store candy. So sweet we could near to breathe it and swell out fat.

It was the noise of the crusher that I hated the worse, a noise that didn't ever ease down; it just went on and on. I tried to make my mind see the rest of the children with Miss Hoe, learning stuff, and also see big Brother Smith in the back of the store, sitting preacher still, and smelling the way he'd usual smell, of catfish.

School could beat down hard on my brain, but cane milling sure didn't. There weren't no thought to it. Only sweat and noise. The faces of the other workers never cracked out a grin. The colored man who worked beside me didn't tell his name.

It was like he weren't even proud enough to share it.

CHAPTER 18

"Fire!"

I'd been too tired to eat supper or help cook much for Papa. Afterward, I'd sunk down on my bed tick, too wore out to even breathe. The yelling work me up.

The voice hollered out again. "Fire! Over to Jailtown!" As I run to the door, I seed old Mr. Witt, one of the pickers, waving his arms and pointing toward town.

Seeing as I hadn't even skin off my clothes before lying down, I run out the door. Huff Cooter was there too, so we rabbit toward town like the road was burning under us bare feet. Ahead of us, orange flames licked upward into the night, spitting sparks like tiny red stars into a black sky.

Huff said, "Looks like it's Mrs. Stout's place."

But it weren't.

As we ran in closer, people were scurrying up and down the street, toting buckets of water. Ever mouth seemed to be yelling an order. Working in close to the fire, I felt the heat of it slapping my face and eyes.

"It's the empty store," I said. "It ain't Mrs. Stout's place. Our school's burning."

A few folks throwed water on the flames, which didn't do more than just hiss out laughter. The fire'd took a real start, so not much short of a hurricane was going to wash it out. People filled their buckets at the mule troughs and then started wetting down Mrs. Stout's store, so's the flames wouldn't jump over and spread.

Brother Smith come.

He just stood in the night, with orange light painted on his black face, and shook his head. His big hands tightened into fists the size of twin hammers.

"It ain't right," Brother mumbled, his voice almost buried in the sharp crackles of the fire. He shook his gray head.

Some of the town women stood nearby, all in bathrobes. I knowed what a bathrobe was, because Mrs. Addie Cooter wore hers every Sunday, all day. She called it her yeller robe, though it sure weren't yeller no longer, but near to egg white, blotchy all over the front with coffee stains.

Miss Hoe come too, in her bathrobe. It was deep blue with a shiny braided belt pulled tight, ending in front with a knot and two hanging tassels of fringe. I didn't know her right off, on account her hair was different. She usual wore it up and wound in a bun, held by long amber pins, but now it was all tumbled down her back and most of it a tired gray.

I run over to take her hand.

"Don't you worry none, Miss Hoe," I told her. "This ain't the end of our school. It's only the end of a building. That ol' store ain't our school. *You* are."

Maybe, I was thinking, my chances for school were burning up too. But at least some of the Cooters might have a shot at learning. It pleased me to figure that maybe a few of us picker kids might make it out of

Jailtown. Didn't look too sunny for Huff, me, or Essie May.

"Arly," she said softly, "do you know what you have become in my life."

"No'm," I said, "I don't guess I do."

"You," she said, "are my rock . . . upon which I will somehow rebuild my school. And don't you fret about missing today. Essie May reported it all to me, about you and her brother, and there are still a few laws in Florida, if matters come to that."

I didn't understand all she was telling me. Hardly any. Yet the pitch of her voice seemed to say that the sun would come up on Jailtown, like always.

"Miss Hoe, I sometimes get to wishing that all this town would burn up, or just sink into Okeechobee and drown. Me along with it."

She looked at me stern. "No," she said, "don't you waste your brain on sour prayers. The world's too sweet for that, Arly, and so are you. Energy your thinking on school."

"I can't come regular no more. Huff and me are standby workers. If'n we git ordered, we go work."

Miss Hoe pointed a finger in my face, a finger that looked brittler than a custard twig. Yet it was straighter than a tiny sword. "Wrong! You *are* coming to school, even if we don't at the moment have one, and you *are* going to learn . . . to read, to count, and to think. You will attend school even if I have to march myself through the swamp in hip boots and drag you out of Captain Tant's cane mill by one ear and the seat of your britches."

I tried to smile about as game as possible. Miss Hoe was staring at the burning store just as its roof rafters caved in and sent another blast of sparky cinders out into a cloud.

"There it go," said Huff, who'd drifted over our way, to stand with our teacher and me.

"Somebody," said Miss Hoe, "didn't approve of our little school. And some hand struck a torch to it."

I looked at her with my mouth open. "You mean a body done this on purpose, to be mean?"

Miss Hoe nodded her small head. "Yes, to be mean. You know, boys, burning down a school house, no matter how humble the structure, is one of the lowest acts that an adult can commit against a child. Or to his town."

"I don't believe it," Huff said. "I just can't swaller that anybody'd do such to my brothers and sisters and to Brother Smith."

Miss Hoe's lips tighted up firm. "We'll need a modest parcel of land. Not much. Only a wee scrap of it. And perhaps with luck, we might get someone who's handy with tools to raise us a structure."

She looked over at Brother Smith, then walked to where he stood. As we come close, he took off his hat. His face looked older tonight, and I could see that our burning school had scorched his spirit near to as black as the rest of him.

"Missy Hoe," his deep voice said, "I be powerful sorry 'bout the store place, and no more school. Powerful sorry."

Our teacher grunted. "Well," she said, "seeing as you're feeling so powerful, maybe you'd work up the strength to build us another."

With a log of a finger, Brother Smith pointed into his own massive chest. "Me?" he asked Miss Hoe.

"You. Could you do it? I don't plan to engage your talents for free, Brother Smith, and you shall be fairly compensated."

"I be what?"

"Paid."

A big grin slowly got born on Brother Smith's face and spread all over his cheeks like a Sunday sleep-late morning. "Oh," he said, "I *do* it, Sister. Do it proud, for free."

Huff jabbed me to my ribs, giggling, on account of Miss Binnie Hoe and Brother Smith looked like brother and sister about as much as a bug and a beef bull.

"Good," said our teacher. "The question still lingering is *where*? We'll have to be cocksure of our ground."

Huff scratched himself. "What's that mean, Miss Hoe?

"It means we can't squat. So if we can muster up ourselves a plot of land, we're in business, as soon as we can beg or borrow the lumber."

We turned away from the burning store, heading home with Miss Binnie Hoe, back toward Mrs. Newell's.

Huff said, "There's a lumber yard in Jailtown."

Miss Hoe let out a snort. "I certainly do not need to inquire as to its ownership, do I?"

"Captain Tant," I said without a think.

But that was when Brother Smith shook his head. "Ain't so," his big voice rumbled. "I heard it told, for sure, that he *don't* own lumber no longer. Something to do with taxes."

"Who owns it then?" asked our teacher.

Brother smiled. "Miss Liddy do."

CHAPTER 19

There was no school.

But there sure was a ample of work. Every morning, right after Addie Cooter would whoa the picker wagon to pick up Papa and the rest of the fielders, Huff and me'd git sent to the sugar mill.

Sunday final come. My daddy slept late, like usual, and so did I. Then I got up, washed, ate, and did me some quiet thinking by the shoreline of the Lake. From across the inlet, near where a dead river knifed back into the thickety green of the gourd vine swamp, I could hear the Sunday morning voice of Brother Smith, humming an old hymn. And I could see him on his pier, a big black catfisherman dotting a pale blue Okeechobee.

Nearby, the water was clearing.

Usual did on Sunday, because during the other days of the work week, the dredger crews stir it into murky mud. Ever since I could remember, the dredgers and their big smokey machines work around Jailtown, trying to unclog an old canal or trench out a new one. Yet old Okeechobee just roll over in the night, and then, come the next morning or the next week, she ooze her way back to normal.

Okeechobee country, I was thinking, weren't too

far from being a fat woman sleeping with bedbugs. Us people were the bugs. She was the lake. Folks, even like the big dredgers, could bite her . . . yet we'd never poke her awake to change.

"I love Sunday," I said to our lake.

Jailtown turned hushy on a Sunday morning. Like the band of Saturday night quit thundering its tune. Even the Lucky Leg was asleep, as if tuckered out from the night before. I s'pose Sunday morning was a sad time for a lot of the workers in Jailtown, because Saturday night wages had a way of jumping out of your pocket by Sunday morn. So people claimed.

Not far away, the giant pink leg stood very still over Miss Angel Free's place of business, like it had never danced at all. The big leg looked too tired to tap a toe.

For some reason, I liked to spend a hunk of Sunday morning all by my lonesome. I wasn't praying, but my thoughts were neighborly close.

I sat there on a cotton bale for a long time, just being a speck of Sunday.

Then I jumped into the water to half-swim and half-wade my way over to Brother Smith's. He fed me a hot white hunk of steamy catfish and boiled swamp cabbage. The two of us, me an' Brother, ate like we was never going to stuff our guts again. Or like Captain Tant was fixing to pass a rule to forbid chewing.

"Good morning, gentlemen."

Seeing the grin on Brother's face, I turned around, even though I already knew the voice of Miss Binnie Hoe. She sure was suited up for Sunday. Her dress was a deep blue, darker than a thunder sky, with lace at the collar and cuffs. The lace was creamy, not white. On her head perched a hat, yet there weren't no bird on it, and no feathers either. To me, her hat looked as if'n it was turned out of mule stable straw. On top, the hat-maker had poked in a few fake flowers that were red, white, and blue.

"You look righteous nice, Miss Hoe."

"Thank you, Arly. Such a sincere compliment is always a welcome."

Brother nodded, as if to say how proper she looked. As soon as he'd saw Miss Hoe coming our way, his hat got yanked off his head by a hurry hand. It pleasure me to notice.

"This morning," Miss Hoe said, "I took myself a walk around Jailtown and inspected the lumberyard."

"Good," I said, knowing that Miss Binnie Hoe was laying a plan in her head to put up a possible new school. She sure had gumption.

"And," she went on to say, "right now, if the two of you will come along as my escorts, we are going to take a stroll together."

"Where to?" I asked her.

"Trust me," she told us. "But please come. I'll need both of you to hold me up if my knees decide to jack." Behind her glasses, her eyes looked bluer and sharper than I'd ever earlier took notice of; our little teacher sported eyes like a pair of Okeechobees. "Let's be off," she said.

Brother didn't ask her where we was going, so I had me a hunch that he already knew. Miss Hoe knew too. Which left only dumb ol' Arly Poole who couldn't reason enough to dump a pebble out a lame boot.

"Miss Hoe, where we be off to?"

"You shall very soon see," she answered me. "As for now, I want you to munch on the mystery. Milk it for all it's worth."

"Sure," I said, knotting up my face. I walked along, milking away, yet coming to no clear reasoning. Miss

Hoe could be worse than a dredge when it come to riling my brain water into a muddy swamp.

As the three of us marched along in the Sunday afternoon, we must've looked like a strange crew.

For one thing, I wasn't wearing no shirt; only trousers that were still soaked wet from wading. Plus, when I'd kicked through the road dust, going to Brother's, my wet toes had gleaned up enough dirt to make my bare feet appear as if I was into earthen stockings. It was sort of fun, on account I'd never owned even one pair of stockings in all my entire life.

Brother Smith was also barefoot. Yet, at least, he was shirted and not bareback, like me. His shirt and trousers was a pale gray, sort of like two big clouds that could pillow around his big body. Miss Hoe'd ordered him to put his hat back on his head so's he wouldn't have to squint. So he final done it.

Whenever I'd seen Brother walking home with Miss Hoe, he'd always take care to walk behind her, on account it just wouldn't look proper for a colored man to walk beside a white lady. Papa usual told me that if'n you be colored or a picker, best we know our place. Still and all, I felt sort of belonging when I'd walk with Miss Hoe. In the rear, I knowed that Brother did too, like he was her watchdog.

I believe Brother Smith would carry Miss Binnie around in her porch rocker chair, wicker and all, if'n she'd asked it of him. He'd follow her, I was thinking to myself, all the way down to Hell or up to Heaven. I'd seen Brother lift up a kitten one time, hold it in the light palm of his giant hand, then touch its head, flower gentle, with the light-colored tip of one of his thick fingers. And that was also how my mind pictured the way Brother'd tote around Miss Hoe, as if she was a parcel too precious to drop to busting.

So the three of us must have more'n looked a mite strange to the rest of Jailtown. Not just to my eyes. As we walked through town, people turned to look at us, even from up on their porches where they'd sat in the shade.

Someday, I was thinking, I'd sure cotton to live myself in a house that sported a step-up porch on its front. Whenever my daddy talked, or dreamed, about his quit-work day, he always promised himself that he'd "ease back on the porch of poverty and salt away worry." That was smack how he'd said it, righteous oft.

Papa spoke about *shade* like it was Heaven.

As we went walking through Jailtown, I still had no notion as to where we were headed. Miss Hoe led the way. Me and Brother Smith trailed a step behind, the two of us walking hip to hip. There sure wasn't one eye that miss us. They all stare.

Soon as we turn the next corner, I knowed.

Ahead was the big white house, the one that people in Jailtown sometime called the Gingerbread Castle. Maybe because the house looked like it got carpented with boards of sugar and roofed with brown molasses cookies. I'd eaten one once.

Brother Smith stopped. "We best go no further, Missy," he warned our teacher. "We go back."

I said, "We can't go to Captain's house."

CHAPTER 20

Brother Smith and I waited.

We couldn't believe seeing Miss Hoe actual do it; trot up on the big porch, ring the bell, and then parade by that big wooden door when it opened. Miss Hoe said something and then went inside. Just looking at Captain's house made me back up a step. Both my lungs held back breathing until Miss Hoe come out again. She wasn't inside Captain Tant's too ample a time.

Out she come, and along beside her was Miss Liddy Tant, looking frail, like she snap easier than a dry twig. Miss Hoe walked down the steps and Miss Liddy come too. She waved a thin salute to Brother Smith and to me. I couldn't make my feet move, though I'd wanted to run away. The two ladies come closer and closer, so near that I could inhale Miss Liddy Tant. She smelled of lilac.

"Good morning," Miss Liddy said in her fluttery voice.

As Brother Smith yanked off his hat, I wanted to hide behind it. Looking down at my ankles, I near to bended down to clean myself.

"We have good news," said Miss Liddy. "You will have land and lumber, at no charge. Not a penny. And if Brother Smith can construct it, you shall have a new school." Smiling, she turned to our teacher. "And it shall be away from Mrs. Stout."

Brother did a little dance. But I still didn't dare to do much more than breathe, without a sound.

"It's about time," Miss Liddy said, "that Jailtown turns into a more fitting monument to our family. A school itself cannot do this. Yet it shall be our start."

Miss Hoe nodded a firm nod. Then she snapped at me sudden.

"Arly Poole, the least you could do is quit staring down at your filthy feet, and say a thank-you to Miss Tant."

My throat choked. All it could do was swallow, and when my mouth final opened, not a word come out. So I tried a grin, and it made Miss Liddy Tant smile too.

"I was shy at that age," Miss Tant said. "And perhaps I shall never become socially at ease. But I intend to attend our business, and try to fill the Captain's shoes."

Miss Hoe thanked her once again, and turned away. Brother Smith and I tagged along behind her. As we got close to Newell's Boarding House, she stopped, turned, and fired us both a pleased grin.

"Tomorrow morn," Miss Hoe said, "lumber shall arrive by mule and wagon at your dock, Brother Smith. I'll be there. And I want you there too, Arly."

"Yes'm." I said. "But why can't we start today?" Brother poked me with his big finger. "Arly, it be Sunday. The lumberyard place be still resting."

Miss Hoe nodded. "Allow me to suggest, by chance, if either of you chance to meet Miss Liddy, that you thank her properly for donating our lumber."

"Maybe," I said, "she done it because her pa order our school burnt."

Miss Hoe shook her head. "No, he didn't. Miss Liddy told me, and neither of you are to repeat a word of this, that Captain Tant is quite ill. Perhaps this explains why his daughter is making her own decisions. Genesis Tant may be dying sooner than his town."

I let out a slow breath. Miss Hoe's words was ample hard to swallow. "Is that his name? Genesis?"

"Yes, that's his Christian name."

"It be a Bible name," said Brother Smith. "First book, my mama tell me."

Miss Hoe's little hand reached out to touch Brother's big one. "Correct. And perhaps the name of Genesis means a new start for Jailtown. A new beginning."

"Sign from God," said Brother, "maybe. Just like you, Missy Hoe. You be a gift to us from the Lord."

As the three of us stood there on the street corner, sunlight sifted down through the green fingery leaves of a giant oak. It certain was, I thought, a Sunday sun. And inside I had a righteous good Sunday feeling.

"Thank you," Miss Hoe said. "So, I guess that's about all we'll do for today. Brother Smith, you might as well return home and go fishing."

Brother yawned. "Well," he said, "I aim to go home and peaceful me a nap." He bowed to Miss Hoe, turned, and amble his big body toward Okeechobee and his shack. As he walk away, his deep voice began to hum a hymn.

"Arly," said Miss Hoe, touching my bare shoulder, "how would you like a present?"

"For *me*?"

"Come along, please."

As the pair of us walked toward Newell's Boarding House, I wondered what kind of a present she had in mind. And then she busted out and let it leak.

"Perhaps you know that Mrs. Newell is a widow.

Her husband died. We had a chat this morning, and it seems that many of her late husband's clothes are still hanging upstairs in a closet. Unused. Verna Newell said it was a shame, and I agree."

"Yes'm."

I didn't dare to speak more. As we reached Mrs. Newell's, my teacher ordered me to hurry around back and wash. There was a bar of brown soap on the pump rail, so I rubbed almost all of myself creamy with lather. Then rinsed off. Standing in the sunshine, I waited to dry my skin proper, then climbed the steps of the out-back porch.

The back door opened and out came Miss Hoe and Mrs. Newell, a lady even smaller than my teacher. Mrs. Newell was holding an orange shirt. It near to blinded me with its pretty.

"Here ya go. Arly," said Mrs. Newell. "My husband was a small man, so maybe you can grow into it."

I had to force my hand to courage up and take it. All I could do was hold the shirt and feel all its finery. Before I could say as much as a sneeze, Mrs. Newell and Miss Hoe snaked me into it, buttons and all. It was a mite too large, but I didn't care a bug's worth about that. "Wow!" I said. "I feel orange all over."

Both ladies laughed.

"Miss Hoe's been telling me about you, Arly. She says you can already read letters and words. Your daddy oughta strut proudly of you."

"I'm proud of Papa too," I said. "Thanks for your shirt, Mrs. Newell. I won't never take it off."

"Except," said Miss Hoe, "for soaping."

I grinned. "Yes'm, I'm to tend it proper."

Mrs. Newell looked sudden sad. "Elbert, rest his soul, cherished that orange thing. Wore it the day we went to Moore Haven, to the fairgrounds. There's a bottom button missing, Arly, yet I don't guess you'll turn fretty over it. I recall how that button come off, the day Elbert and I went . . ." Her voice trailed off to empty. "Come inside, the both of you," she said. "I could do with a cup of tea."

I'd never been inside a house so grand as Mrs. Newell's. There was even boards and cloth to walk on. In the hallway, I didn't even dare to move for fear I'd nudge something over to breaking. There was nobody in the parlor. All the boarders must've been out or upstairs, sleeping their Sunday.

"You got a *piano!*" I said.

Mrs. Newell nodded. "Elbert use to play it, evenings. I can't as much as even finger a single note. It's been closed for years."

I ventured a step closer to the piano. "Golly," I said to Mrs. Newell, "you should hear Knuckle Knapp play *his* piano machine. Have you ever been inside the Lucky Leg and heard. . . ?" My hand flew up to cover my mouth.

Miss Hoe smiled. "Knuckle Knapp is not the *only* piano player in Jailtown." As she said it, her fingers wiggled as if trying to loosen their age.

I saw Mrs. Newell look at her. "Do you play?"

It took Miss Binnie Hoe less than a breath to open that machine, sit on the three-legged pie, and bless the keys with music. She even sang a song, called *When the Organ Played at Twilight*, warbling out the words in a birdy voice.

Mrs. Newell and I clapped.

Miss Hoe crooked a skinny finger at me. "Come over here, Arly." As I stepped closer to the piano machine, Miss Hoe stood up from the stool, ordering me to sit down on the round wooden pie. "You're too high," she said. "Up."

Soon as I stood up again, she spinned the seat around in circles, sat me down and laughed at the way my face must've looked. I was shorter. Then I spinned myself around, one time, just for the fun of it.

"Arly," said Miss Hoe, "you may touch the keys."

Being right cautious, I press down about seven or eight, yet no music pop out.

"Harder."

"No," I said, "I'll bust it."

She lifted my hands and then pushed them downwards on the keys. It made noise. But what I sounded be more like mud than music.

"It ain't too ample pretty," I said.

Miss Hoe smile at me. "That, my boy, will brighten as soon as I teach you which notes to play." Taking my pointing finger, she rest it to one of the white keys. "If you can count up to eight, you can play a piano."

"Honest?"

"It's easy as eating. One, three, and five blend together to rhyme a chord. Press these three."

I did what Miss Hoe tell me. She was right, like usual. My three notes rung out like sisters.

"Good," said Mrs. Newell.

As I played the three notes again, I grinned. It was a clean feeling to listen up to how my own hand could press out music. So, without even as much as a prod from Miss Binnie Hoe, I slided my arm sideways to press down three new notes. The same kind of sound jumped out; only this time, the three sisters sang a mite younger. Higher up.

The music made me laugh.

Without any more teaching words from Miss Hoe, I rested my other hand on the man keys, the ones with the deeper voices. Then I just let my thumb monkey around until I found which note got along friendly with my three sisters. Like he was their daddy. Soon as I'd pressed a more cousinly sound, I looked up at Miss Hoe to read her smile.

"I played a family," I said.

"Oh, Arly," said Miss Hoe, standing behind me with her skinny little arms around my neck, "you're the morning of life."

CHAPTER 21

Brother Smith worked ample quick.

Miss Liddy Tant had made good on her promise, and the boards arrived, smelling cleaner than my new shirt. Miss Hoe said that our land would be near Brother Smith's place, so that he could guard off trouble. She also claimed that Miss Liddy would give strict orders to Mr. Roscoe Broda that our new school place was to git left alone.

We worked a whole week on it.

As we pounded in the final peg, I stood back to look at what all of us had put up. It sure didn't favor Captain Tant's house. Part of it looked crooked, and it listed to one side, but I felt proud about it fit to bust. Maybe, according to Brother Smith, our little school shack might even git slapped with a coat of whitewash, soon as he could locate the time.

Miss Hoe sighed. "She'll do."

I saw Brother Smith take off his hat, then shuffle a step of two closer to our teacher.

"Missy Hoe," his deep voice near to whispered, "I got a surprise." Without another word, he melted into his shack and then come back out again, toting a long whitewashed plank.

I wondered what his single board had to do with our new building, yet I sure didn't have to ponder too long.

"Please," Brother Smith said to us helpers. "Y'all best close up your eyes. And turn about, hear? No peekers."

Eyes closed, we all turned our backs to the school, listening to Brother's busy hammer, wondering why Brother Smith had started to hum a hymn to the beat of his pounding.

"Now," he said, "you can look."

Turning around, I saw his fresh board, shiny white, with letters of bright blue painted across it. He nailed up a sign over the doorway. Miss Hoe said the words:

BINNIE HOE SCHOOL

Brother Smith's teeth all smiled wider than the keyboard of Mrs. Newell's parlor piano. "I hereby ordain our school after my teacher." Then he throwed his hat up into the sunshine.

"Welcome," said Brother. "You be home."

To me, Brother Smith looked older and tired out. The hammer slipped from his hand. Looking down, he didn't seem to muster the strength to bend over to fetch it up. I picked it up for him.

Holding the hammer, Brother Smith looked up at the sign.

"Hope I letter it right, Missy Hoe. I practice like you tell me, with my Bible. But I cheat some. I ask Mrs. Newell to write down your name for me, and spell out school."

Miss Hoe couldn't say nothing. So she only kneeled down on the sand, her little hands covering her face. We waited for her to speak up, which she final did. "I guess," she said in a husky voice, "that I'm about the luckiest lady in all of Florida." Standing up quickly, she said, "Brother Smith, seeing as you were my first pupil, I think it would be proper that as we enter our school, you lead us the way."

The big man shook his head. "Don't guess I'll be coming no more, Missy Hoe. School ain't no place for some old blacky like me. It belong to the children now. I take up too much room." He looked square at our teacher. "You understand Jailtown."

Miss Hoe nodded. "I do."

Taking one more look at the little school he'd built, Brother turned and walked slowly away.

We went inside.

Our teacher asked us to sit on the new benches and stood straight in front of us. It was a time before she could speak. "What you just heard," she told us really soft, "was a sacrifice. I know that's a big word, but Brother Smith is a very big gentleman." After she said it, Miss Hoe bit on her lip.

Miss Hoe showed us a book, telling us a whopper of a surprise. It was a book donated by Miss Angel Free herself, even though Miss Hoe had lost the pool table game. The book, as Miss Hoe told me and the Cooters, had been delivered to Newell's Boarding House late last night, by Mr. Knuckle Knapp, the piano player at the Lucky Leg. So, right then, Miss Hoe started to read it to us all.

It was about a boy whose name was Tom Sawyer and I swallowed down every word she read. She showed us the pages and let each one of us hold it in our hands. But the sticky part was when we had to take turns reading it out loud. It be painful going. Huff Cooter read so powerful slow that he took angry and ripped out one of the pages.

Miss Hoe didn't look too pleased.

"I got me a temper," Huff said.

Our teacher scowled at him, long and hard. "We all have tempers, Huff. But destroying a book is akin to burning a school." She put the page back inside the book.

"Are you riled at me?" Huff asked.

"Plenty. But I'm more than angry at Jailtown and Shack Row. Never at youngsters who now have a chance to become more than pickers. It's no sin to fail, Huff Cooter, but tearing a book isn't a proper way to thank Brother Smith."

Huff looked down to study his dirty feet. "No, I don't guess it be. I'm sorry."

As I sat there, I was busy recalling one of the things that Brother had mention this past week. While we was fitting boards to the side of our new schoolhouse. "A good carpenter," Brother Smith had told me, "measure twice and saw once."

I figured Brother had measured a few matters in his head, counting the lean turnout at our school, and how so many families keep their kids away. Maybe some of the white folks never forgive Brother for being on his own, not living in Darky Town but at his dock place on the lake. So, just today, he sawed hisself off from schooling, even though he'd a hanker to come and learn.

Thinking on it turned me glad that I'd throwed the dime back to that plume hunter. I'd measure and saw too.

After school let loose of us, I walk back to Shack Row, left the Cooters and set myself down at our doorway. Shack Row sure didn't shine like Mrs. Newell's house, or Captain Tant's. Our shacks weren't white. They was all gray boards, rotted with weather, most of them loose and curling away from their frames.

But it was home.

There was seven shacks on our side of the road and six across the dirt wagon road that divided the two rows. Thirteen shacks. Somebody said one time that thirteen weren't too lucky.

"You're right," I said aloud.

It was a sorry thought to want to settle in Shack Row forever. Yet I couldn't leave Papa. He'd be too skittery to follow. Across the road, a family named Yurman lived. Clete Yurman had tried to run off that one time. Roscoe Broda brung him back with a rope knotted around Mr. Yurman's neck, telling him he owed too hefty a debt at Mrs. Stout's trading store.

It was sudden after when Bess Yurman, their eldest girl, left home and went to work at the Lucky Leg for Miss Angel Free. She never come back again except once, when her ma slapped her red-painted mouth. Then, as Bess run back toward Jailtown, her ma had throwed herself down into the dust of Shack Row, screaming, and biting her own hand.

Nobody talked about Bess Yurman. It was like she fade off into a workday mist. Worse than dead.

I scratched my body. Remembering stuff about Bess commenced me to itching. Because it was Essie May Cooter's turn coming up, and maybe she'd try on Miss Angel's fancy bonnet one more instance. Thinking on it hurt me inside.

My nose sniffed.

Somebody, in one of the shacks, was boiling up turnips. It certain was a smell that belonged to a Shack Row supper. It meant that the picker wagon would be soon coming. I'd have to go see if there was any fire in our cookstove.

Getting up, I took myself uproad, beyond the last pair of shacks, to wait for Papa. A few other kids were there too, like usual.

We didn't take long to wait.

Around the bend, the picker wagon busted through the scrub and into sight; Addie Cooter sat up front on her bench, driving. The four mules come toward me with their heads hung, plodding along to the growing rattle of the wagon.

"Howdy," I said to Mrs. Cooter.

She only nodded, looking too sweaty and too tired to let loose of reins or speaking. The men looked even worse. Most of them was burnt a reddy raw from the all-day sun.

Nobody said anything. I saw Papa help old Mr. Dinker Witt down over the tailgate. One of the mules let out a bray. Addie cussed her.

Papa looked at me.

Yet he didn't smile. Instead, he held a hand over one side of his face, as if trying to cover himself over. I didn't have to ask. He'd probable got clouted by Roscoe or a field boss for sneaking into shade or to fetch a swaller of water. His other hand held his empty noon bag which hung down limp and wore out. It was near as dusty as Papa. Nobody spoke a goodnight to no one else. There was just the usual silent march through the grit, down between the tiny houses of Shack Row. Gray men to gray homes.

Mr. Witt stumbled and fell.

Papa reached him first, hefted him up, and we helped him home between us. I wondered how olden Dinker Witt was. His hat had fell off and his white hair was wet with work sweat. Actual, he was soaked clear through his shirt. So was Papa.

"Tomorrow," I said to my daddy, "you best rest. I'll go pick in your place."

"No," he said. "You got school."

CHAPTER 22

I tended Papa.

As he was too tuckered to even wash, I dipped a rag from my old shirt into some stove water and wiped him warm. He was breathing like it was work to pump his lungs.

"Papa," I said, as I tried to ease him on his bed tick, "we all readed in school today. Miss Hoe owns a book about a kid called Tom Sawyer, and I was reading it out loud."

He flashed me a weak grin. "That's good, Arly. Ya gotta master it all. Every lick. I don't want ya to . . ." His cough didn't let him finish. Papa only lay back and closed his eyes. "Melons," he whispered. "I bet I picked ample to feed all the world and half the stars."

"Are ya hungry? I'll fix ya supper."

All he did was shake his head. "I ate myself melons enough to bust open. Broda caught me and give my back a smart with a stick." Papa chuckled. "But he don't make me puke it all back, no sir."

He slept. Dan Poole's body curled up into his own shadow and never even twitched. When I touched him, it was like resting a hand to our cookstove. Summer hot. Opening his eyes, Papa looked at me, and told me how happy he was that I'd got a new shirt, the orange one I'd had on me for days. Then he rested hisself quiet.

Addie Cooter sent Delbert over with a fresh melon, and I told him to be sure to thank his ma. But I couldn't eat even the first slice of it. To enjoy it didn't seem fair to my father. Fact is, I didn't want anyone to eat another melon. Not anywhere, because of the long day that Dan Poole had sweated through.

So I picked up the melon, went outside our shack, and throwed it hard against a big oak.

Looking up through the leaves, I wondered what it would be like to live away up on a star. Planters, up yonder, probable raise melons too. And, I was thinking, I bet they got Pooles to load 'em to a wagon. Mules to haul away. Just maybe there was a boy up on that star place who just busted a melon, like me, because he don't no longer want to be hisself . . . yet there ain't nobody else to be.

"Don't cry," I told the boy in the sky. "Please don't let no sorry flow, or the hurt to bleed into your bones. Stand up proper and tell yourself lies. Same as me. Tell your picker pa that life'll ripe sweeter, even if you know it's rotten wrong to hope it."

My neck hurt.

But I couldn't quit looking to the stars, because they seemed to wink down to me, to Arly Poole. It made me wonder, when the earth's so hot and gritty, how a sky can look so holy clean. It looked as if God had just soaped it righteous. I leaned against a cypress, feeling the bark press into the back of my orange shirt. Quickly, I pulled away. The shirt felt as though it lingered to Mr. Newell. Still his. But not me.

"I don't got to be owned by anybody. Not even Captain or Broda."

Walking over to the trunk of the big live oak, I

grabbed a wet hunk of melon and ate it. And hated myself for eating it. But I was hungry. One hunk of dirty melon didn't cool me a whole mite. I spat out a seed. It lay on the sand, in moonlight, looking like a sad little canoe, going nowhere.

The smell from the turpentine mill drifted in, strong and sharp, with a sting to it that was near to whiskey.

"I'm Arly Poole," I said. "This is Florida, and I live in Jailtown which ain't the whole dang world. Stars," I said, looking up again, "don't belong to Captain Tant."

Thrusting both hands into my pockets, I walk along through the darkness toward Jailtown. I wanted to see Miss Hoe. When I got to Newell's Boarding House, there she was, sitting in one of the rocker chairs up on the front porch. As she notice me coming, she stood up and raise a hand.

"Arly? Is that you?"

"Yes'm."

"Come sit."

I bounded up the steps. Then bended down to wipe the boards clean of sand that scuff off my bare feet, and sat down real careful.

"Thank you for coming to see me."

"You're welcome."

The front door was open and a smell of fresh biscuits crept out and into my belly. I wanted to tell Miss Hoe how hungry I was, yet held off. To get someplace empty, Papa always said, just weren't proper manners.

"I really like *Tom Sawyer*," I said.

"Good. It's a book that takes to people, too."

"Reckon."

I rocked my chair again so it'd keep paced with

Miss Hoe's pulling like a team of wagon mules. "Living," I said, "is sort of like rocking."

Miss Hoe looked at me. "How so?"

"Well, the way I figure it, just when you got everything moving forward, it all stops, and back you go."

She laughed. "Arly, how I do envy the way you phrase things. Somewhere, in your background, there just had to be a lyrical Irish poet. Or perhaps an English one."

"Thanks. But you're dead wrong on both counts. All I got in me is . . . picker."

Her little hands slapped the chair arms. "Nonsense. There's so much in you that Heaven alone couldn't hold it all. So much more than Jailtown or Florida. You are America, boy. Why, you're the eagle, the flag, and President Coolidge . . . all wrapped in one gift."

I stopped rocking. "You know President Coolidge?"

She smiled. "Not very well. But I know who he is, the way he knows who I am. By that, I mean that Mr. Coolidge wants our Congress to cut the taxes we little folks pay. I heard tell that a United States senator had the gall to accuse Mr. Coolidge of trying to save money."

"And what did he say to that?"

"President Coolidge told him that he wasn't trying to save money. He was attempting to save *people*."

I sighed. "You know, maybe I just might sort of like Mr. Coolidge."

Miss Hoe let out a healthy laugh. "You would. Better yet, I know for certain sure he'd like you."

I picked at a sore on my toe until Miss Hoe scolded me to quit.

"Does he ever come to Jailtown?"

My teacher's frown faded away. "Well, I don't imagine he'll be here too soon."

My hand cuffed a biter bug. "I guess if'n Mr. Coolidge come to Jailtown, he'd stay at Captain Tant's and Miss Liddy's."

I saw Miss Hoe shake her head. "No, he might not. My guess is that if Calvin Coolidge came to visit Jailtown, he'd bunk in here at the boarding house." Miss Hoe smiled at me. "Arly, *you* could be president someday."

Hearing her say it almost tumbled me off the rocker chair. "*Me*?"

"Honestly. I love America when she elects . . . little people, like Cal Coolidge. He was born in a very small town, you know, away up north on a Vermont farm. That's why he knows about hard work and the folks who bend to it."

"You told us about President Coolidge in school. But I don't guess I can remember anything famous that he ever said."

Miss Hoe slapped her knee.

"That's his beauty, Arly. At last we have ourselves an honest farm boy who doesn't speak too much or too often. And if he decides to run again, in nineteen hundred twenty-eight, he's got my vote."

I grinned and then felt my face fall to sober. "Papa don't vote at all."

She touched my hand. "But *you* shall. You'll be heard. And better than only being listened to, you will also be watched and heeded."

Her hand floated up to touch my head.

"You always do that," I said. "When we git talking, you reach up and touch my ears. How come you do it?"

"Because."

I shook a finger at her. "That ain't a proper answer. Leastwise, that's what you always tell us to school."

"Very well. Because . . . if you'll permit me a deep breath, a rural teacher, like myself, works in an educational dungeon. In the dark, Arly. Sometimes the darkness lasts for years and years. But then, just when she almost concludes there is no light, a wee little spark ignites. Have you ever looked up to the sky on a misty evening?" Miss Hoe pinched my elbow. "It's all up there, my dear. Then, the breezes clear away the fog and out pops the first star. That one sparkling Arly Poole that I know could shine beyond clouds, darkness, and Shack Row."

I was sort of surprised to see Miss Hoe jump up from her chair and move to the porch railing. She pointed up at the sky.

"Always look up, Arly. Even if you trip when walking, look upward at the sky and all its lanterns."

CHAPTER 23

I skip happy all the way home.

Shack Row weren't sleeping, like usual. Instead of folks resting supper, inside their shacks, I saw people standing in clumps outside our doorway in the dark.

Coming closer, I could hear Addie Cooter crying. Nearby was Essie May, holding little Florence and staring my way. Turning my head, I saw old Mr. Witt limping toward me, holding out both his arms like he had something to speak out.

"Arly?"

I didn't answer up because his face seem to want to tell me the all of it.

"It's your pa," Mr. Witt said.

"What's wrong?" As I asked the question, my whole body started to heat, like I'd sudden took a fever. Saying no more, I run inside our shack to where my daddy lay on his tick.

"Papa?"

There was no answering. Just silence. As I kneel down to shake his shoulder, I felt Mr. Witt enter our shack to come up behind, resting his hand to me. "He give out, Arly. I come across to see him and found Dan like he be now. Clean gone."

"*Papa?*"

More people crowd up closer to our door, and I could hear little Delbert Cooter say, "I want to go see the dead man. Let me go see Mr. Poole."

"Please hush," his ma said.

Mr. Witt spoke. "He be, Arly. Dan Poole's left us."

"No," was all I could say.

"I figure it was his poorly lungs. All that crop-dusty poison. And I be powerful sorry, Arly." His hand pat my back. "We're to miss old Daniel."

Somebody lit a candle. Then I saw Papa's face, a raw red, like usual, from all his hours, his days, an entire lifetime under sun. Except for Sundays, there weren't been as puny as a leaf of shade to cool him or allow him to rest under. Bending over, I wrapped both arms around the thin body, to rock him gentle, holding his head to my shoulder. The stubble of his beard rub scratchy against my cheek, yet it was an honest feel, rough, with no quit to it. Like each tiny whisker stuck out brave to know it'd be a final chance to stand proud.

"Papa," I whispered to his ear, "I never got you no rocker chair."

Looking down at his face, I could see that his eyes were near closed. He was resting. His field work was over. The tore rag of his shirt smelled of melons, sweat, and black soil. There was still grit on his hands.

"Somebody's went to fetch Brother Smith," Mrs. Cooter said.

Mr. Witt kept patting my shoulder. Leastwise, his old hand moved on me, even though I couldn't feel nothing on my side of it. Mrs. Witt was near too.

I couldn't make myself turn Papa loose or lie him back down to his tick. So I only kneel in the candlelight and rocked him. With my hand I tidy his hair so he'd appear handsome to the Heaven folks. He'd already gone. The man in my arms weren't no longer Dan Poole. Maybe the angels wouldn't bother to ask if'n he was only a picker. Eyes closed, I somehow saw Papa all dressed fine in a new white suit, with a hat to match that would shade his head. And white shoes.

"Papa, you look so proper. And I be so proud of you. They don't work nobody in Heaven, and God won't charge no shack rent. You don't have to cough up a penny to live there. It's all free. All clean. And most of it's in the shade."

I thought I heared him breathe. Opening my eyes, I knowed that I'd thunk wrong. Papa weren't to breathe no more. Or choke his crop dust.

"Brother Smith's here," Essie said.

I was still kneeling on the dirt of our shack floor when Brother come to us. For some reason, I didn't have to look over my shoulder. Then I feel his big hands on me, hefting me up, as if ordering me to turn Papa free.

"Come now, Arly," he said. "We help."

Us pickers had our own graveyard. Out back. Not too fancy a place. No markers with names on them. And the crosses fell over in the rainy season, even though the kin of the dead tried to keep the crosses stood up. Dinker Witt and Mr. Yurman had a hole dug, and we walked to it. The grave weren't ample more than a knee deep. Brother Smith carried Papa in his mighty arms, lighter than he'd burden a half-growed child. Essie May line Papa's grave with fresh greens and fern to fashion a bed for his resting. Jackson and Delbert add some flower petals. Mrs. Witt come with a small rag pillow, handmade, with fancy sewing on it in color yarn, to place under my daddy's head.

Looking down at him, I was thankful that tomorrow there'd be no run for the picker wagon. Or no half wages.

Bending, I folded his rough hands over his skinny chest the way people are supposed to do. It would be the last thing I'd do for him, so I took a ample time doing it, locking his fingers, just the way he'd say a blessing over our beans. Then I nod to Brother Smith.

"Brothers and sisters," his deep voice said. "We gather to bury Daniel Poole, a man who be neighbor, friend, and a daddy to his Arly. All his life he work on dirt. Now he sleep in it. He *good* white man, Dan Poole. Live proper. We all look to a young colt, a boy that he raise up, to see goodness sweet as apple. Jesus love Dan, because He love us all who got dirt to our hand and clean in our heart."

Brother stretched his big arms toward the sky, closing his eyes, and smiling. As I started to shake some, Mrs. Cooter held me close to her, supporting me up. She felt warm and good clear through.

"Ain't no cukes to pick in Heaven," said Brother. "Only be sunshine and moonlight and angels to sing sweeter than whippoorwill. Ain't no sweat up in the yonder, or mean-mouth folk to yell angry. Everyday be Sunday peaceful. Dan, he already know. Already there. Angel folks now washing him clean with virtue so he look his best to greet the Almighty."

Leaning close to Addie Cooter, I prayed that all the words Brother said would blossom true. Even if'n no, I felt thankful that he'd spoke it out so shining.

I was sort of surprised when I saw Brother Smith stuff a hand inside the front of his billowy shirt and pull out his little Bible. Behind him, Mr. Yurman lit up a pine torch and stepped in closer to shed light.

"I now read," said Brother, "from the First Book of Moses, call Genesis." He paused. Then, bowing his head to his open Bible, his thick fingers sort of blessed the crispy pages as if he loved each one. "This," he said softly, "be my mama's Bible, and it say like so." Brother readed slowly. "In the beginning, God create the Heaven and the Earth."

That was all he read. Brother close his Bible, stoop down, and toss one handful of dirt onto Papa. "Amen," he said.

"Amen," everyone said too.

"Dan Poole," said Brother Smith, "you got a Genesis now in Heaven. A new beginning. So don't you fret no more. We look to young Arly and do for him proper, hear?"

Papa hears, I was thinking, trying to stand proud and not shake too ample much.

More petals got sprinkle all over my daddy's body to quilt him. Two of the pickers work spades to begin the covering as Addie Cooter turned me away. Even so, I wheel around one last time, trying to catch one final look at the only other Poole I ever knowed.

Brother Smith come over to me.

"Thank you," I told him.

His big hand took my shoulder. "Arly, you best spend a life just exact the way Dan wish for you."

One by each, the people of Shack Row come to me, putting their arms around me. Yet I couldn't feel nothing except empty. I was a bucket with its bottom tore out, and all of my innards was draining from me.

Brother Smith was the last one.

As the two of us stood alone behind our shack, I looked up at his kindly face. God, I figured, had to favor Brother Smith. He too would be a strong and gentle giant that a person could turn to for solace. Brother's big hand rest light on my shoulder.

"You ain't alone," he said. "Nobody be. Because

there's a Almighty away up in the yonder, smiling down at you, and wanting to grow you up tall and sturdy, the same way He do for a young cabbage palm. He'll keep on sending you sunshine to dry a washing, and rain to water your thirst. The Lord be a bigger brother to you, Arly, than this old fisher ever hope to be."

I nodded, but it weren't much more than a slight bow of my head.

"Thanks for coming, Brother Smith. I don't guess nobody hereabouts could get proper buried without you to say words."

With his arm across my back, his hand on my far shoulder, Brother turned me around, and together we walked to the road side of our shack, to its only door.

"You best go inside and try to sleep." His hand touched my face. "I be here outside at your doorway, like a old guard dog. Arly, I'll be right nearby until you go to sleep. Hear?"

"Yes. I hear."

Lying inside the shack on my tick, I listened to the deep voice of Brother Smith humming a hymn. No words. It was only a light breeze of a tune which seemed to whisper to my ears and to close my eyes.

I feeled like a sick hound, remembering Dan Poole and everything he'd told me, and how hard he'd sweated all his life as a picker.

With every breath, I could still smell Papa.

CHAPTER 24

Morning come.

Somehow, during the darksome, I'd fell asleep listening to Brother Smith's gentle hum. He was gone, and outside the shack the first early gray of a new day was arriving.

"Papa," I said, with no thinking. "You'll miss the picker wagon."

Only then did his dying live again. Across the single room of the shack lay an empty tick, mussed up against the board wall, looking gray, alone and cold.

"He's no more," I said.

Wherever he was, I wanted Dan Poole to know that I weren't about to quit learning. Because that was all he wanted. My schooling and a ticket out of Jailtown.

"Arly?"

Somebody said my name. Hearing it, I jumped up quick and hurried to the door, thinking it was Mrs. Cooter. I was wrong. It was Miss Hoe.

"Oh, Arly . . . I just heard."

"My daddy died last night."

"I'm so sorry." As she holded out both her hands, I took them. "The pair of you seemed to be so deeply proud of each other. So very belonging."

"Yes'm."

She hugged me very gentle. "Brother Smith came over to Mrs. Newell's before I was even up or dressed," she spoke into my ear. "He could hardly speak. I guess he'd waited outside, holding his hat, until Verna Newell rushed out. Then he told the two of us . . . *Brother Poole be dead.* That's how he said it, Arly. Softer than a prayer."

"Thank you," I said, "for feeling grief."

Releasing me, holding my shoulders at arm's length, she studied my face. "Believe me, I really do. But what a gift you'll someday give your father. You were his hope, Arly. His escape and his dream. I read it all on his face the day I stepped off the gangplank of the Caloosahatchee Queen and saw him shove you toward your . . . famous lady."

Miss Hoe tried a smile.

"Papa wanted me to git choose for your school."

The teacher held my face in her little hands. "You *have* been chosen, by Brother Smith, by all your Shack Row neighbors, and by God. To learn, to love, and to grow." She shook her head at me. "No hatred, Arly. Not even a wee lick of it. It would be wasting a good brain."

"I'm plenty scared, Miss Hoe. Because I got me a hunch that maybe Papa and me still owe at Mrs. Stout's trading store. On Saturday nights, us pickers got to report there, to settle up. So if'n I owe, I can't never leave Jailtown. Mr. Broda will fetch me back with a rope to my neck, like he done Mr. Yurman."

"No," said Miss Hoe. "He won't." Her mouth was set grim tight as she spoke it.

I shook my head. "You be new in Jailtown. They got rules and orders for Shack Row people. If'n ya cut loose, you maybe don't git no shack to roof over you.

And they'll put you on half wages whenever you stir up trouble. You can ask Mr. Yurman if you don't believe it. Nobody run away, Miss Hoe, because they dassn't dare."

"Arly," she said, "come with me."

"Where to?"

"I'm taking you to Mrs. Newell's."

"No!" I near to hollered at her. "I'll miss the picker wagon. Mr. Broda will put my name on his roster board, to take Papa's place. I gotta go pick."

Miss Hoe shook her head. "That's not true. You're coming along with me, and that's all there is to it."

The two of us near trot through the Okeechobee mist on our way out of Shack Row as we headed for Jailtown. Once we'd leg it to Mrs. Newell's, my teacher sent me out back to wash myself clean. After that, Mrs. Newell fed me full on stew and two glasses of sweet milk. I tried not to gulp it all in too fast, yet I did. Both of the ladies sat to watch me while I ate.

"Arly, I have a cousin in Moore Haven," Mrs. Newell told me. "His name is Mr. Alfred Bonner, and he's a schoolteacher.'"

Dribbling milk down my chin, I wiped it on my sleeve and grinned. "I already got a teacher. Fact be, I got me the best doggone schoolteacher in the all of Florida." I winked at Miss Hoe.

"Thank you, Arly," Miss Hoe said. "But Verna and I have talked it all over, and Mr. Bonner knows you're coming."

"Run away?" As I asked the question, the hot stew bubbled up from my belly and I could taste it again, in my gullet.

"You're getting out, Arly Poole," said Miss Hoe. "And you will be the first of many to follow. My flagship. There won't be any picker wagon looking for you, or any bloodhounds on your trail."

"Amen," said Mrs. Newell.

"I can't leave Essie May," I said. "Because if I do y'all know what'll happen to her. She'll wind up going to live at the Lucky Leg Social Palace. And it ain't right. I got feelings for her."

Miss Hoe nodded. "I understand, but Essie May might be older than you are, in some ways."

"Maybe so," I told her, "but maybe no. Both of you ladies is real kind, so I don't guess I can sass you none, but I'm not always going to be a kid. I'm close to being a man. All men ain't as big as Roscoe Broda. Papa was a small man. So is Mr. Witt."

Standing up, Miss Hoe started to rub her hands, as Mrs. Verna Newell cleared the table, run water into her sink place, but didn't use it much. She walked around the kitchen, going nowhere, and the two ladies sort of looked at each other without speaking.

"Arly," said Miss Hoe after taking a deep breath, "it's all arranged. Brother Smith is going to help us get you away. He's in on it too. But you've got to trust us, all the way, and believe in what we're doing. If you drag your feet . . ."

My fist hit the table. "I'm sorry," I said quick, "but it couldn't be decent for me to leave Essie here in Jailtown. It just wouldn't seem righteous."

"You are very young, Arly," said Miss Hoe. "Perhaps older than Verna and I imagined, yet you're still younger than you are judging to be. Give yourself this chance to grow, Arly. You can't grab a rosebud and force it open into a rose. You need time to blossom into manhood."

"Essie May's already a woman." As I said it, I could hardly hold back telling what I knowed about

Essie and Roscoe Broda, and the thought of it soured my insides, like I might lose up all the milk and stew. "Someday," I said, "Essie and me are going to be one, flying together like two white gulls."

Miss Hoe shook her head. Sitting down at the table, she reached out to touch my hand.

"Moving on," she told me, "often entails a leaving behind of treasured things and cherished people. When I came to Jailtown, I left someone behind, a person very dear to me. Yet I had to tighten my will and do it. Because it needed doing." Miss Hoe sighed. "Oh, there's such a selfish streak in us schoolmarms. We never expect our kittens to ever grow up and become cats."

"I ain't nobody's kitten, Miss Hoe."

"No indeed, you certainly are not." She smiled. "Least of all mine."

I stood up. "Thanks for the meal, Mrs. Newell. Believe me, I ain't never ate so good in my whole entire life. But I'm going back to Shack Row and locate Essie May. On account it be ample better to face sorry matters and not just run away like it don't be worth a bother."

"Think on it, Arly," Miss Hoe said. "Verna and I won't push you. You'll have to make up your own mind what to do."

Nodding, I thank both the ladies once again, and left, running all the way from town and back to Shack Row. I never stop running until I pulled to a whoa at Addie Cooter's place.

"Essie?"

Mrs. Cooter come to the door, holding little Florence in her chubby arms. Her eyes look red and her face swollen, a blushy pink.

"She ain't here."

"Where'd she go, Mrs. Cooter?"

It was a while before Addie Cooter could answer

me. All she done was look off toward Jailtown, her chin trembling. "Last night, after we buried your pa, it must've all took place. Maybe I was too tired to wake up to reason, on account I'd had trouble with the mules. And this morning, Roscoe Broda told me all about it."

"About what?"

"Essie's gone. I ain't got her no more."

"Where is she, Mrs. Cooter? Where'd she go?"

"She . . . she's with Miss Angel Free. Roscoe's seen her there, late last night, and told me this morning with a smarty-mean grin on his face. Huff's gone too. All I got left is Delbert and Jackson and little Flo."

She slump to the door stoop of her shack, cradling Florence in her arms, hiding her face into the child's hair, her big body shaking.

"I'm . . . all shame. Don't know if I can ever eye decent people again, or face the world. God, please help me keep the three I got left. Help me, Lord, please . . . please . . ."

As I touch Addie Cooter's shoulder, efforting to comfort her some, I could hear a horse nicker. Turning about, I saw somebody cantering my way on a bay gelding.

Roscoe Broda.

CHAPTER 25

"**A**rly Poole."

The way Mr. Broda spoke my name made my spine rattle, like he was telling me that I belong to old Genesis Tant, now and forever.

"Boy," he said, "you been hiding off from me all morning, and so you're on half wages for today and tomorrow. Hear?"

"I hear."

He spur his gelding close to me, so near that I could smell the sweat of horse breath. Foam from its mouth spatter me. "You got shack rent due come Saturday night. Maybe it won't be so pig simple for you to tally up."

"I know that," I said. "I'll work it clear."

Broda took off his hat to wipe his face with a sleeve. "There's ample more you don't know. Dan Poole become so illy useless to me that he'd worked on half wages better'n a week." Broda pulled out his pocket watch. "You got five minutes to report to the cane crusher. Pronto. Or git dragged there like a stuck hawg." As he spoke, I noticed the coiled rope which he looped around the horn of his saddle.

My legs steadied real sudden. "I'll go," I told Mr.

Broda, "but first I aim to visit the Lucky Leg and fetch Essie May back home. She don't belong there. Essie's only a kid."

Broda's eyes narrow. I could tell by his look that he figured maybe Essie told me about what he'd done to her, and I'd tell Miss Angel. Or maybe even Miss Liddy Tant. His look made me study the ground.

"Damn you, Poole."

The rope hissed out so fast that I hardly saw it coming. All I felt was a loop tightening around me, pinning my arms to my body. I got jerked off my feet and my face was sudden eating dirt. All I knowed was that I was getting dragged along the sandy road, hearing the hoofs of his horse, and Mrs. Cooter's screaming for it all to stop.

He didn't stop. Not until I got drug through the fanpalm prickers and sandspurs for what seemed to be near a lifetime. But then the rope eased to quit, leaving me lying in the marsh muck, hurting all over. Broda's hands was on me, claiming his rope. "You're now at the cane mill, boy. Fastest trip a picker ever took to work." Broda laughed. "Now git up and report to Mr. Lem Rathaway inside."

He kicked me, real hard.

"From now on," he said, "best you forget all you heard about me. You're to forget the Cooter gal and also forget about school. Fact is, the only thing you *remember* is that you're a picker, boy. A picker."

Broda spat in my face.

Mounting his gelding, he recoiled his rope and then rode off in the direction of the produce fields, leaving me standing ankle-deep in the black mud. I couldn't breathe. It was like Roscoe Broda's noose was still around me, and my arms smarted from the rope burns. My new orange shirt was now a tore-up rag. But all my pain melt away gradual, until I couldn't feel nothing alive in me, like I was some old limper of a dog.

Then I heared a voice. "Git in here!"

As if in a dream I stumble toward the cane mill to report. When asked what my name was, I couldn't speak it out right away. Finally I did, and they hand me a broom to sweep up the spill. The noise from the crusher was fearful loud. Picker! Picker! Picker! After a while, though, I couldn't hear it, because a dead soul can't listen.

Seeing as I hadn't brung a noon bag, I didn't get to eat a midday meal. My gut surely ached hollow by whistle time. I headed to Shack Row in a daze, feeling nothing, not even the sand under my toes.

I couldn't eat.

So I just hided myself in a corner of our shack, behind the cookstove, praying for dark. All I could hear was the picker-picker-picker noise of the cane crusher, even though it'd be shut down until morning. For near all-day I'd worked for half wages which wouldn't cover my shack rent.

My gut felt empty, yet the thought of even chicken turned my stomach. I still feeled Broda's rope around me, dragging me through all the thorns, stumps and muck.

But then I started to remember Papa, and how proud he was that I was getting some schooling, and about Mrs. Newell's cousin in Moore Haven who'd maybe take me in. I'd earn my keep. Because I weren't about to burden somebody who be a schoolteacher. Seems like if'n he was Mrs. Newell's cousin, he'd be a decent sort of a gentleman, like Mrs. Newell who give me a shirt.

I stood up.

"Arly, it's near about time you gathered your guts together and quit taking it all on the chin."

As I walked to the doorway, Shack Row was tuckered out quiet and rested down for keeps. So I headed myself toward town, knowing exact where I'd be going, right to the Lucky Leg Social Palace. Maybe I could rescue Essie May Cooter before she become another of Miss Angel's fancy ladies.

Outside of the Lucky Leg, as I was hiding myself in the bushes, I could see into one of the windows and its lace curtains. The music of Knuckle Knapp's piano tinkled through the open window. Used to be, I liked hearing him play, but not no more. The piano music sounded like a devil's hymn.

I saw Essie May Cooter.

After first, I didn't know it was Essie. Her hair looked different, lighter in color, almost tow. And her clothes was now satiny yellow, to match her new hair. It seemed that Essie May Cooter weren't no longer the same girl, because on her face was color paint, and her mouth was redder than a rose. Yet, to me, she looked like a dead bird, one that'd got gunned down somewhere, to frill up a lady's hat.

To see Essie like so was sadder than finding Papa dead. Dan Poole had his life, but Essie wouldn't never have hers, except for socialing dredgers at the Lucky Leg for the rest of her time. The girl I was watching through the window now be somebody strange to me, like she fell from a distant star, someone I no longer knowed. I ached to touch her face one last time.

She looked at me sudden.

Then, with a signal of her head and eyes, she moved toward the side door. Hoping she'd meet me there, I went too, and sure enough Essie come outside and whisper my name. I was thankful that it was dark and she couldn't see how beat-up I was.

"Arly?"

I went to her. She smelled like a evil flower, sweet and sickening as the stink from the cane crusher at the sugar mill. Her perfume near to made me gag.

"It's too late, Arly. Please don't scold me none. Just tell Mama how much I love her and y'all. Honest do. But I had to get out'n our shack, or smother. Miss Angel says she knows a doctor man, over in Moore Haven, who'll fix my belly so's I don't ever born no kids." Her chin tremble. "Don't carry no hate for me, Arly. Please don't."

"I can't, Essie."

"We had feelings, Arly, you and me. But I ain't never again going to feel deep about nobody. Miss Angel says that for a spell I won't have to social no men. My job's to parade around and be bait, to sucker the sports inside to git serviced upstairs by the older ladies."

Holding my hands over my ears, I couldn't listen to no more. It hurt too much. Looking at Essie was like watching somebody step on a flower.

"We could run away, Essie May."

She shook her heard. "No, on account I made up my mind. I'm out of Shack Row for keeps. I ain't to become another Addie Cooter and sweat like a mule. My belly won't never swell up around a baby. Not yours, not nobody's baby. Because babies, Miss Angel says, is little more than nails in a poorhouse coffin. So don't pity me, Arly. I made my bed."

Taking my face in her hands, real gentle, Essie May Cooter kiss both my cheeks. Her lips were fluttery soft, like the wings of a broken butterfly.

"Take care now, Arly Poole."

Somehow, she seemed older, as though Essie was

twice my age, and already knowed so much about the upstairs life, things I'd yet to discover.

"You take care," I said, trying to hold my feelings back from the brink of crying.

Turning away, she went back inside the red door, and didn't once look back to watch me wave.

"Good-bye," I told Essie, saying it to the girl who'd sat in school with chalk dust on her fingertips, a young lady I'd danced a hundred years ago. I'd known Essie May Cooter ever since I could remember. Her and Huff was the first kids I'd ever played with, and all of the Cooters was a part of my entire life. Yet somewhere I'd always guessed she'd become a woman before I'd git to be a growed-up man. Walking away from the Lucky Leg, I kept saying, "I'll come back for you, Essie," even though I couldn't begin to guess how.

I knocked at Mrs. Newell's door.

But it weren't Mrs. Newell or Miss Hoe who answered. A big dredger come to the doorway, staring at me through the screen. Turning around, he shouted up the stairs. "Miss Hoe, there's a visitor here to see ya."

"Thank you. I'll be right down."

The dredger left me standing on the porch, wondering how I had the strength to pace back and forth. I'd worked most of a full day on only what Mrs. Newell give me, early this morning. My stomach was already complaining too. It seemed a long time before Miss Binnie Hoe final come to the door.

"Arly!" As I turned to face her in the porch light, her mouth flew open. "Lord, what happened to you?"

Being tired, hungry and heart-broke over Essie, I'd forgot that I'd been rope-dragged by Roscoe Broda, scuffed up and tore by the torns and prickers. Looking down at myself, I saw that my clothes was near to rags.

"I'm sorry to look so shameful. Please don't let Mrs. Newell see my shirt. It'd hurt her feelings."

Coming out the door, Miss Hoe hurried to me, threw her arms around me, real snug. It made me sort of back away.

"Careful," I told her, "I'll git you dirty as me."

"Oh, you precious Arly Poole."

"Essie May's at the Lucky Leg," I told Miss Hoe. "And it's hurting her ma something awful. Me too. I can't hurt you, not on purpose, but I don't guess I can handle life much longer."

Miss Hoe shook her head. "No, Arly . . . the answer isn't dying. It's living."

"Yes'm. So now I'm ready to do whatever, like you want." My body started to shake.

"Come," she said, "and we'll soap you clean."

CHAPTER 26

They washed me.

I was too tired and tore up to squawk. Mrs. Newell and Miss Hoe spooned food into me, put some stingy iodine and bandages on my gashes, and then dressed me in more of Mr. Newell's clothes. Neither lady seemed to give a hoot that, except for the sudsy soap lather, I'd been near to newborn naked. Both ladies were too busy to look.

"Mrs. Newell," I said, "I'm dreadful sorry about Mr. Newell's orange shirt getting so ripped."

"Oh," she said, "they's plenty more."

They led me upstairs, to a tiny little room and ordered me into a real bed, to sleep on clean cloth for my very first time. Sure felt strange. They quieted my shaking, placed a soft pillow under my head, and left. Just as I was going to sleep, I overheard Miss Hoe say something to Mrs. Newell that shook me awake sudden quick.

It was about Huff Cooter.

Over in the swamp, Broda's men caught up to Huff, dragged him back to Jailtown and tossed him in a jail cell. Tomorrow, according to Miss Hoe, he'd start work on the highway crew, in chains. It all had to do with his mother owing at the store. Blinking, looking at the clean white ceiling overhead, I thought I'd best see what I could do for Huff. Maybe he was alone in the dark, behind bars, scared and crying.

Hungry too.

So later, when I heard Mrs. Newell's grandfather's clock strike more times than I had fingers, I figured it was midnight. Getting out of bed, sneaking down the stairs, I helped myself to some sticky rolls, three oranges, a doughnut, and some prunes.

I left by the back door.

Staying in the shadows, I moved slowly through Jailtown in the direction of the jail. The building was only one story high, no upstairs, and the barred windows were below ground level, in pits. So I snuck along, hugging the outer concrete-block wall, stopping outside each window.

"Huff . . . you in there?"

No answer. Only a muffled voice that sounded like it belonged to a very old person. Whoever he was, he coughed.

"Huff . . ."

I hit it lucky.

"Arly? Is that you out yonder?"

"It's me. Here, I brung ya some eats."

Hands reached through the bars. He ate the doughnut in about three or four snaps. Mumbling how good it all was, Huff ate an orange, a sticky bun, and a couple of prunes.

"Miss Hoe knows you're inside," I told him. "She'll do all she can to spring you out of there."

"It don't matter, Arly."

"Why don't it?"

"Because . . . because Essie's gone to reside at the Leg. That you possible already know. So tell Miss Hoe to work on Essie May's problem. It's a whole worse'n mine."

"I will."

"Never mind on me, Arly. I didn't take to schooling much as you. Maybe I'll be a picker, or work with Ma seeing to the mules. It was dumb to run off. That old swamp back yonder is one spooky hellhole. Murky water, green slime, moss hanging down like ghosts in the night. All them frogs drumming at you from all sides."

"Gators?"

"Only saw one. Arly, I near to stepped on him. He give out a hiss loud enough to scorch a man's mind to crazy. So I turned tail and retreated, only to meet Jim Tanner's dogs. One bited me fearful. I'm still bleedy."

He ate more prunes, spitting the pits out one-by-one through the bars and into the dusty sand.

"Huff, I'm leaving too."

"When?"

"Tomorrow night, Miss Hoe says."

"How?"

"Don't know yet. But it'll probable be to Moore Haven . . . at Mrs. Newell's cousin's place. We gotta keep in touch, Huff. We're pals. So sometime, ask Mrs. Newell at Newell's Boarding House exact where I'm at."

Huff laughed. "Poor old Arly Poole. He's so simple he don't know where he is yet."

Both of us were giggling. But right then, I stopped, because there was a noise behind me, coming from the roadway, toward town.

"Dogs," said Huff. "You best scamper."

I touched his hand, jumped out of the pit, then run, hearing one of the hounds bugle, followed by a man's deep voice. "Vernon, you hear anything?"

Another man answer in a high-pitch voice. "Nope,

I didn't hear a cussed thing, but my dog certain did. Looky them ear."

"Which way?"

"Well, maybe over along them bushes by the jailhouse wall. Let's go see."

Again I ran. Behind me, two dogs tune up their bugling like they'd treed a coon. Outside the feed store stood an empty ammonia barrel. It stunk to glory. Sharp fumes that smart your eyes. But it was the perfect hiding place. Made to order. There weren't a dog alive that would keep his nose anywhere near ammonia. Holding my breath, and nose, I crawled inside the barrel, closed my eyes really tight, and prayed.

The dogs come.

Vernon and Deep Voice come too, letting the dogs sniff around. I could hear their panting. But one whiff of ammonia and both dogs turned tail. One even whine. Then another dog come back to brave one more intake. Maybe he smell *picker*. Mr. Roscoe Broda always claim that there be a stench on us Shack Row people. The dog stay for so long that I was crazy for air. Yet if I breathe, I'd cough. That'd bring the guns.

Ripping off my biggest bandage, the one still soaking with iodine, I held it to where I could see a dog's snout through the widest crack between the barrel staves. One whiff. The strong medicine smell of iodine caused the hound to yelp, and run away.

"It ain't nothing," Vernon said to either his dog or to his friend.

They left, arguing.

As I crawled out the barrel, I took in air, filling my lungs and making me feel alive again. The men and their dogs were close to the jailhouse wall, patrolling, so there was little hope in going back to Huff. Yet I still was too frighted to stray too far away from the ammonia barrel, even though my eyes were stinging.

All along, I was hoping that both Miss Hoe and Mrs. Newell were sound sleepers. If either lady woke up in the night and went to check on me, they'd possible turn to worry.

My progress back to Newell's Boarding House was slower than torture. No point in making any noise. I'd been careless with Huff Cooter. The two of us must've stirred up enough racket to turn the dogs pesky. Or perhaps one of the hounds sniffed the air, caught my scent, and then started fighting his leash.

"Vernon," I could hear one of the men say, "best we check down under the boat dock."

Their voices fade to silence.

But still I stay in the thickest and darkest of cover, seeking deep shadow, mindful of the overhead moon. As I walk on tiptoe, I watched where I was stepping, fearful that my foot could rattle a tin can.

By the time I'd made it back to Mrs. Newell's rear door, my body was close to tuckering out. My eyes were saggy and I still smell of ammonia. While sneaking in the door, through the kitchen, I heard the clock strike.

Bong! Bong!

The sound near to stopped my heart. But I figured it wouldn't wake up Mrs. Newell as she'd heared it strike the hour for a spate of years.

In bed, I couldn't sleep. So I toss around some, trying one hip, then another. My eyes were close, yet my memory kept seeing one sight, over and over.

Huff's hands through the bars.

143

CHAPTER 27

I final slept.

In my dreams, however, I kept hearing the bugling and sniffing of those redtick hounds. Plus hearing the voices of the men with guns.

Broda's men.

Captain Tant's men.

I could smell the hot breath of Roscoe Broda's horse, feeling his rope around my neck, dragging me back to Shack Row. His voice cut me like a whip. Also in my dream Knuckle Knapp was playing the piano. The music drifted to the jailhouse from the Lucky Leg Social Palace.

Worst of all, the painted face of Essie May Cooter kept staring at me, from inside the Lucky Leg, looking out. But there were bars at the window.

"Essie," I shouted in the night. Yet as I yelled, no words come out my mouth. Only a empty echo of silence.

Essie May Cooter could no longer hear me.

She was gone.

The sorry dreaming come to a finish, waking me awash with sweat. My nose could still smell the iodine on my cuts and rope burns.

At first, in the morning light, I didn't know where I was. There weren't no shack roof overhead. No roof at all. Instead, a big white square with no holes in it. Didn't even look like any roof I'd ever saw. Rolling over, my body hurted and smarted.

Iodine was near worse'n injury.

I could still taste Roscoe Broda's spit on my face. Tobacco spit. Brown and sour. It seemed to stink of crushed sugar cane, mule dirt, and the dusty sand of Jailtown.

I got up.

My clothes were different. Then I recalled last night, and my brain crept into the daylight too.

Somebody knock. The door open a crack, just enough to allow me to see Miss Hoe, smiling. She sure did own a good smile, bright and shining, the same way she look on the Sunday when she paraded down the gangplank off the Caloosahatchee Queen. Like she could rinse all the dirty off Jailtown and buff it into a sparkle.

"Arly," she said, "you're already up."

"Yes'm."

"I have good news." She took my hand and held it. "Verna Newell received a letter from Moore Haven, from her cousin."

"The schoolteacher man?"

"Correct. And I've called on Miss Liddy Tant. She has promised to see that Mrs. Stout clear the books, and properly. The Pooles no longer owe at the store, not for rent or for anything else."

I couldn't speak. A "thank you" wouldn't even come out my mouth, the way it ought.

"You're leaving Jailtown, for good. Mrs. Newell's cousin and his wife once had a son. He'd be about your age, had he lived. So they want you for their own."

It couldn't be true what Miss Hoe was saying. Nobody runs away. I kept remembering Mr. Clete Yurman and how he got dragged back to Shack Row, behind horses. And then working on half wages. But the face of Miss Binnie Hoe was looking at me straight, and I knowed she wouldn't make up a story. It sure weren't easy to believe they be people in the world like a teacher.

"I never knowed my ma," I said. "But I hope when she was alive, that Mama be somebody like you."

It was all I could say to Miss Hoe. Inside, I wanted to tell her that I needed a person to love, to hold close, somebody more than Addie Cooter or Essie, even closer than Brother Smith. Maybe, instead of a wife, I only wanted a mother.

"I have some sad news too," Miss Hoe told me. "It seems like they caught Huff Cooter and brought him back."

"I know. I took him food."

Miss Hoe blink her eyes. "That was foolish. A very risky thing to do." Then her face turn soft again. "Yet I'm glad you cared enough to be so brave. Now then, until nightfall, you're not to budge from this house. When the hour comes, I shall be leaving with you."

"You're going to Moore Haven too?"

"No. Only you. But we mustn't risk our chances. Liddy Tant warned me about some of the cruel things that happen here after dark. Even to someone she once loved."

Around noon, Miss Hoe somehow got Huff Cooter out of jail and returned to his mother.

Mrs. Newell fed me again. Twice. Once in the later morning and then again before sundown. We'd spent the afternoon fitting more clothes on me which Mrs. Verna Newell rolled up for me into a bundle. Inside, she and Miss Hoe tucked some brownie cookies, and something else. It was a thing real special . . . Miss Hoe's book about that boy named Tom Sawyer, which she give me because I'd once give her a snake fang toothpick.

Miss Hoe also give me a clean white handkerchief so's I wouldn't no longer blow my nose on the ground.

Soon as it reach dark, I said good-bye to Mrs. Newell, thanking her again and again for all her doing.

"Bless you, Arly," she said.

Miss Hoe sneak us both out the back door of Newell's Boarding House, and together we walk through the shadows toward Brother's boat dock. I took notice that my teacher took me clear across the other side of town and nowhere close to the Lucky Leg Social Palace.

I stopped.

"Miss Hoe, I gotta do something before I leave Jailtown. One more thing. Somebody I got to go visit."

Miss Hoe looked alarmed. "Who?"

"He's at Shack Row. He's been there all his life, so I don't guess he'd be nowhere else."

"Very well, but I don't like it. Let's hurry."

Somewhere, off in the Florida night, a dog barked, and my body turned wet. Walking quietly through the stand of custard apple trees along the lake shore, we made it to Shack Row. I took Miss Hoe's hand so she wouldn't stumble in the shadows. Behind our shack, the only place I ever called home, the moonlight lit up a mound of fresh sand. Miss Hoe waited behind as I kneeled down.

"Papa," I said, "maybe it ain't right, but I got to leave you." I looked up, then down again at his grave. "There be trees above you, Papa, so you'll rest in shade."

Stretching out a hand, I grabbed some of his grave dirt and poured it into my pocket. It was all I could take with me of Dan Poole.

"I'm ready," I told Miss Hoe.

"And I'm glad you came to say farewell to your father."

At the boat dock, Brother Smith was waiting for us, holding a Coleman lantern. When he spotted us hurrying his way, he smiled, and come to greet us. "Be best we take Arly by water," he said to Miss Hoe, "on account Mr. Broda's gunners might lug him back, like they done to other runaway people."

Reaching a hand inside his shirt, Brother fetched out his mother's Bible. Opening it gentle, he cracked it almost in half, like he didn't care which page lay open, then pointed to something with a big finger. The pages yellowed in the lantern light.

Miss Hoe squinted. "Isaiah," she whispered.

Brother nodded. "Swords into plowshares. Arly, your fighting time be ended. Now comes the time of planting, to harvest." He flashed a grin at our teacher. "That be all I remember Mama tell me. Once I fought. Now I harvest my fish."

"Bless your heart, Brother Smith," Miss Hoe said. "I'm glad you're reading your Bible now."

Brother shook his gray head. "No, not hardly, as my sight is too olden. Be a shame to waste a Bible under closing eyes." He handed his Bible to me. "Arly Poole, you keep it. Thataway, it'll git readed proper for years to come."

"Thank you, Brother," I said. "But I couldn't take it. That just wouldn't be right. You give me a lot already."

Brother Smith pressed it close to my chest. "Take it along. It be all I got to give you. Don't got nothing else to match your worth."

It weren't easy to thank Brother Smith for being

such a good brother to me. All I could do was look up at him. His grin told me that he understood.

"A long time back," Brother spoke in a low voice, "I hated all white folks with a hot fury, like they's be a fire inside my belly. Then I see a little white girl fixing to drown. For a breath, I figured I'd just allow her to sink under, for old Okeechobee to take her deep. But it weren't right. So I dived in to save her. Turned out, she be a Tant child. Captain Tant's only." His hand rested light on my shoulder. "On that day, I rescue more'n Miss Liddy. I save my own soul."

Right then, I knew what Brother Smith was telling me. To forgive.

"Here," said Miss Hoe, stuffing a scrap of white paper in my pocket, "is the letter and the name of Verna's cousin, with the street where he lives in Moore Haven. His name is Alfred Bonner."

I nodded. "Yes'm."

"Boat's ready," said Brother Smith. "Arly, say a proper good-bye to your teacher lady."

How, I was wondering, would I be able to make words out of all the feeling inside me? Not even the gentleman who'd wrote the book about Tom Sawyer could do it decent enough. All I could do was hug her and hold her close to me, knowing that I'd always remember her goodness. Her little body was shaking, so I patted her shoulder, the same way you'd do for a baby.

"Arly," I heared her whisper to my ear, "let me tell you again . . . you're my morning of life . . . that one wonder of a child that every teacher dreams of discovering. And there you were, ready to blossom in Shack Row. Now go forward, Arly Poole, and don't look back."

I nodded silent.

It come to me what I could say, but I'd save it until the boat would be away from the dock. Only one word, but she'd be pleased that I could master it, and use it proper. It be a word to claim that I weren't no longer bitter about nothing or nobody. Only thankful.

Brother Smith loaded me and my clothes bundle into his little sculler boat, sat facing me, and start to work the oars. The bottom of the boat felt gritty and damp beneath my bare feet. Sitting on the stern seat, I twisted around so that I could wave to Miss Binnie Hoe. In the night, she stood on the dock, a small woman growing smaller with the first pull of the oars.

I waved. So did she.

Then I spoke the word I was saving to tell my famous lady because she would understand. A name to hold in her heart. Even if I couldn't no longer see her face, I knew my one good-bye word would make her smile all over.

"Genesis."

THE END

Postscript

Today, here in Florida, there are thousands upon thousands of little Arly Pooles.

Their names are Marita and Pasco. In many cases, this is the only name they know. They move as pickers do, from field to field, grove to grove, from one Shack Row to the next. They wear rags. Their little faces stare, without expression, from the cracked windows of old school buses, no longer yellow, that will never unload at a school.

These children are thin, and hungry.

And ours.

R. N. P.

How to Help

There are several worthy organizations in Florida that deserve our salute, and our support:

Florida Association of Community Health Centers
Community Health of South Dade
East Pasco Health Center
Florida Community Health Centers
Florida Rural Health Services
Redlands Christian Migrant Association
Ruskin Migrant and Community Health Center
Southwest Florida Health Centers
West Orange Farm Workers Health Association

If we all help, we can make sure that children as well as vegetables are growing, and greening, in our Eden—Florida, our home.

Robert Newton Peck

point®

Other books you will enjoy, about real kids like you!

☐ MZ43469-1	**Arly** Robert Newton Peck	$2.95
☐ MZ40515-2	**City Light** Harry Mazer	$2.75
☐ MZ44494-8	**Enter Three Witches** Kate Gilmore	$2.95
☐ MZ40943-3	**Fallen Angels** Walter Dean Myers	$3.50
☐ MZ40847-X	**First a Dream** Maureen Daly	$3.25
☐ MZ43020-3	**Handsome as Anything** Merrill Joan Gerber	$2.95
☐ MZ43999-5	**Just a Summer Romance** Ann M. Martin	$2.75
☐ MZ44629-0	**Last Dance** Caroline B. Cooney	$2.95
☐ MZ44628-2	**Life Without Friends** Ellen Emerson White	$2.95
☐ MZ42769-5	**Losing Joe's Place** Gordon Korman	$2.95
☐ MZ43664-3	**A Pack of Lies** Geraldine McCaughrean	$2.95
☐ MZ43419-5	**Pocket Change** Kathryn Jensen	$2.95
☐ MZ43821-2	**A Royal Pain** Ellen Conford	$2.95
☐ MZ44429-8	**A Semester in the Life of a Garbage Bag** Gordon Korman	$2.95
☐ MZ43867-0	**Son of Interflux** Gordon Korman	$2.95
☐ MZ43971-5	**The Stepfather Game** Norah McClintock	$2.95
☐ MZ41513-1	**The Tricksters** Margaret Mahy	$2.95
☐ MZ43638-4	**Up Country** Alden R. Carter	$2.95

Watch for new titles coming soon!
Available wherever you buy books, or use this order form.

Scholastic Inc., P.O. Box 7502, 2931 E. McCarty Street, Jefferson City, MO 65102

Please send me the books I have checked above. I am enclosing $ _____
Please add $2.00 to cover shipping and handling. Send check or money order - no cash or C.O.D's please.

Name _____

Address _____

City _____ State/Zip _____

Please allow four to six weeks for delivery. Offer good in U.S.A. only. Sorry, mail orders are not available to residents of Canada. Prices subject to changes.

PNT691